A Hero Rising

Aubrie Dionne

This book is a work of fiction. Names, characters, places, and incidents are the product of the author's imagination or are used fictitiously. Any resemblance to actual events, locales, or persons, living or dead, is coincidental.

Entangled Publishing, LLC
2614 South Timberline Road
Suite 109
Fort Collins, CO 80525
Visit our website at www.entangledpublishing.com.

Edited by Kerry Vail
Cover design by Heather Howland

ISBN 978-1-62266-843-4

Manufactured in the United States of America

First Edition February 2012

To my husband, Chris, for watching all those crazy zombie movies with me over and over again.

Chapter One

Left Behind

Clutching his retractable cable, James lowered himself down the glassy surface of the high-rise as the wind stole the warmth of the sheets he'd just left behind. He glanced at the fluttering curtain three stories above his, wondering how Mestasis would feel when she awoke to an empty bed. He detached his grappling hook and slipped inside the balcony of the building, fast as a diving raven's shadow.

If only I could stay longer. If only things could be different.

His wristband flashed another message.

If you don't get down here within the hour, I'm coming to look for you.

The thought of Dal stumbling through the abandoned subway by himself sent adrenaline rushing through James's veins. The lower levels had been dangerous since Dal was a boy, but with the introduction of Morpheus, the desperate scavengers had grown into vicious savages.

James typed a message back, hoping Dal would believe him.

I'LL BE THERE. STAY WHERE YOU ARE.

Mestasis will have to understand.

He took an elevator down as far as it worked, holding onto the slim hope he'd have a chance to give Mestasis a decent good-bye later. The elevator creaked to a halt and the doors parted to a corridor lit by one flickering bulb. Crumpled rags and broken vials dusted with the dried, silvery sheen of Morpheus lined the floor.

The lower levels.

No one decent ventured down this far, so the government didn't find it necessary to cover low level repairs. It would only bring up gangmen, like himself, to the upper levels. *But some of us are good. It's those Razornecks that give gangs a bad name.*

He jogged to the end and slid down a plastic recycling chute to Level Five. The chute ended with a rusted metal grating piled high with cracked bottles and compacted cans. He kicked out the grating and emerged on a stairwell landing. Cracked bottles rattled around him as he shuffled through the debris to Level One, the place where only the bravest, or craziest, treaded alone.

The scent of dank air and old garbage wafted up from the moldy floor. It smelled like home. He'd been away too long. James ducked through a shattered window to an alley between the buildings.

Twilight spread through the sky, stretching the shadows of lumbering heaps of old mattresses, broken ionizers, and tattered plastic bags. Using the darkness as his cloak, he climbed through the debris and checked over his shoulder. The alley lay as silent as a wasteland. Residents had boarded most of the windows to keep out thieves, but apartments lay empty and dark as deep space.

Three windows down, a small child with wispy black hair peered out, clicking off a flickering light stick. The child disappeared as he approached. James reached in his pocket and left an orange on the sill before ducking away.

A stone stairway loomed at the end of the alley like a mouth to the underworld. James slipped down a corroded railing to an old subterranean transportation system once used by his ancestors in the days before the mega-high-rises and the elite's reign of the upper levels.

Pitch-black oozed from under the brick, and his hair glowed neon green as the darkness enveloped him. The radiance was just enough to light his path, the permanent dye a trademark of his gang. James picked up his pace and jogged along the tracks, approaching a thick cement door with graffiti scribbled in hasty strokes.

He raised his hand to knock, but he paused with his fist in midair. Shuffling echoed down the track to his right. No one could see him entering the Radioactive Hand of Justice's underground facility—he had to find out who had found him and make sure he or she wouldn't talk.

James slipped past the door and tiptoed closer, his hair casting light a few feet around him in every direction. No one could sneak up on him.

Was it Dal?

"Hello?" His voice echoed down the shaft.

The shuffling continued and James froze, listening for footsteps. The motion sounded more like the fluttering of bats than any tapping of feet. Bats didn't scamper on the ground.

Someone snickered and then sucked in a long breath

before cackling lightly like a witch in a fairy tale. The person smacked his lips together. James narrowed his eyes.

Oh great—some desperate savage, looking for anything he can sell for Morpheus. Maybe I can knock him out and leave him on Level One where he came from.

"Stay where you are." James's voice was deep and authoritative.

The shadow moved toward him in a flurry. The smell of mold and rotten food clogged his throat, and James resisted the urge to gag. Where had this man been?

"I said, stay where you are."

He blinked, and when he opened his eyes again, the figure had scuttled ten feet closer, arms writhing like snakes in the air. James stumbled back. He'd only seen them from the safety of the city walls before.

Oh geez. A moonshiner gone over the edge.

Moonshiners got their superhuman speed from the drug Morpheus, a chemical mined on the moon. Too bad the drug also caused an insatiable urge to kill. James had heard about the moonshiners who lost their minds from stories the city wall guardians told. He reached for his laser, but the man scurried closer like he was in an old movie on fast-forward.

James had enough time to deflect the moonshiner's jaws with his elbow as the man's face came into view. Sunken cheeks held shadows where the chemical spread like ink underneath the skin. James pushed back against the man's weight, throwing him off. The moonshiner lunged at him before James could recover, scratching his chest with jagged fingernails that had grown so long, some of them were curled. James kicked him in the gut, but it did no good. The moonshiner was past the point of reacting to pain.

The man pushed James over and fell on top of him, jaws clacking an inch from his face. James held him back with one arm while the other worked his laser out of its holster. The man's eyes had turned into black holes, the pupils bleeding over the whites to give him a fiendish glare. Strands of hair shed from his scalp, trailing down his arms to tickle James's face. The moonshiner's head was disproportionately larger than his body, as if his skull had begun to grow and change, morphing into an oval.

Yeah, this moonshiner is past gone. Must have been using for years. Why didn't the guard take him out when he entered the city?

James yanked his arm free to fire his laser directly into the man's midsection, and the moonshiner fell back with the force. Jumping to his feet, James raised his laser again. He shot the moonshiner three more times in the chest and shoulder, but the man scrambled up and kept coming.

Panic rose inside James in a riptide. Would the moonshiner never tire or die? Hissing with a black-toothed grin, the man crashed into him, pushing James into the wall and knocking the air out of him. Even the guy's teeth looked different—inhuman, pointed like a shark's incisors. James banged his head against the cement and dropped his laser. He struggled to focus as the world warped.

Would he die like this? Torn to pieces by a druggie monster?

No. Too many people needed him. He had to see Mestasis one last time.

James fought, wrestling the moonshiner to the ground. He rolled over and stretched his hand out, clawing for the laser. His index finger curled under the trigger and he brought the gun up in one swift motion. The man caught his wrist, and James struggled to point the laser at the moonshiner's head.

Just a little lower.

The moonshiner opened his mouth, and a dry, rasping

voice whispered, "Aliens. They left something behind on the moon."

"What the—" James hesitated, and the moonshiner lunged for his neck. He fired at the man's head and the moonshiner stilled and collapsed.

Pulling himself up, James tried to calm his racing heart and think straight.

Where did this moonshiner come from? What brought him into the tunnels? And what aliens?

James didn't have time to decode the strange riddle leaking from a moonshiner's crazy mouth. Worried about Dal, he rushed to the cement door and banged five times: two quarter notes followed by three eighth notes. If anything had happened to them while he was away, he would never forgive himself—even if it meant regretting his last hours with Mestasis.

The door creaked and three laser barrels poked through the crevice. James held up his hands. "Whoa, guys. It's only me."

An older man with a tuft of white hair stared back at him. Relief shone in his bright blue eyes.

"James, we thought they got you."

"The Razornecks, the government, or the moonshiner I just blasted in the tunnel?"

"Any. All three." Dal clapped him on the shoulder and led him inside while two guards stayed behind to close the entrance. Even though the cement locked in place, James had a hard time letting go of the encounter outside. The hideout didn't feel safe any longer.

"What's happened while I've been on the upper levels?"

"Nothing good." Dal led him through a tunnel to the concrete bunker underneath the subway system. He talked over his shoulder as they hurried down the steep incline.

"As you can see from your new friend lurking by the door, moonshiners have infiltrated the sewers, climbing through miles of pipeline to rise to the lower levels."

"Yeah, the one I met smelled like death."

"That's not all. A crazed mob of 'em storms the city walls as we speak. Guardians pick them off with gallium laser blasts, but they don't have enough firepower to keep them back."

"Hold it now." James stopped midstep and Dal halted beside him. "The walls are five feet thick. No way the moonshiners can get through, even if they clawed with their fingernails all day long."

Dal shook his head slowly. "They are, and they will. Some of them still have part of their brains left, and they've been tossing hypergrenades at the cement."

James scratched his head. "Jeez, where have I been?"

"Making sure three hundred of our people got the hell out of here." Dal squeezed his shoulder. His voice was shaky. "Did it take off?"

James shook his head. "Not yet. But it's on schedule. I'd like to see it leave, so if we could hurry…"

"I understand." Dal clapped him on the back. "Just checking to make sure my grandkids made it safely."

"If you'd tell me why I'm here, I could make sure of it."

"Yes, yes. Let's go. There's something I have to show you."

James followed him to a low-ceilinged room lined with wallscreens displaying input feeds from all over the world. In the dim light, Dal's wispy hair glowed like James's, giving the old man a halo of green, otherworldly light.

Dal sat in a rolling chair across from a circular desk and gestured for James to follow. James waved his offer away. "I prefer to stand." Every second counted. He knew Mestasis wouldn't wait for him—shouldn't wait for him. She'd probably think he'd left to avoid such a painful good-bye.

"You may want to sit down when you hear what I'm about to tell you." Dal gave him a sad smile.

"I can take it." James's gaze passed from a riot in Mexico to a volcano warning in the Hawaiian Islands to flames consuming Utopia, the last giant greenhouse that fed all of New England and the surrounding states. "No place is safe, is it?"

"No." Dal pressed a button, zooming in on the ruins of Utopia. "One of our spies got a lowdown on the Razornecks' counterattack…"

"A counterattack? Already? I thought most of the Razornecks died in the blaze?"

Dal shook his head. "They have cells throughout the city, and they're all seeking revenge."

James ran a hand through his hair. "What is it this time?"

"Assassination attempt. Governor Ursula Grier. They found out she was the one who ordered the counterstrike on Utopia after they took it over."

That's why Dal had called him down so quickly. "Should I organize a team to stop them?"

Dal clicked a button and the screen changed. "No."

"No? What do you mean *no*?"

"The Radioactive Hand of Justice shouldn't get involved in government affairs. Besides, she's got enough guards and artillery to defend herself, and in two days' time, she'll be leaving on the *Heritage*, along with the other heads of state. The government in New York will be nonexistent." The inevitability in Dal's voice sent a shiver down James's back.

"They're going to abandon us?" Government officials didn't just get up and leave their posts. This was serious.

"It's their only choice for survival." Dal clicked on another screen, bringing up a meeting of world leaders from at least five countries, all sitting around a circular table.

"More problems?" James studied the screen, recognizing the faces: most from the World Coalition. "What are they saying?"

"They want to nuke the areas with the largest concentration of moonshiners before the mobs grow out of control. As it is, the force outside these gates could rip through this entire population within days."

"They're targeting us? Citizens?"

"Bingo." Dal sighed. "We think this bunker would hold during the attacks, but we're not sure we could live here until the fallout dispersed. We have the fluorescent greeneries, and the stocks are piled high, but it would take years for the radiation to return to safe levels."

"Not acceptable." James shook his head, refusing to resign to such a fate. "There has to be another way."

"There is." Dal's fingers flicked across the keypad and a picture of a gigantic chrome hull loomed over their heads.

"The *Destiny*."

"Wait a second. We were deemed unfit for the *Expedition*. Who's to say whoever built this ship wouldn't conclude the same thing? I'm sure they have their own people to transport."

"The project was abandoned three months ago. It's not finished. The biodome hasn't been completed, and it isn't stocked with enough energy cells. It won't be able to fly us on a hundred-year journey, but with a little work it could get us off this doomed rock."

James put his hand on his hip. Every paradise planet he'd heard of was hundreds of years away, which could only mean one thing. "You're thinking Outpost Omega, aren't you?"

"It's the biggest space station within a parsec of Earth, fully equipped with biodomes, solar panels, and energy cells."

"It's also the most important and the most heavily guarded. They'd never let a ragtag army like us live there.

Only government workers are allowed to set foot on it."

"Then we'll take it by force."

James exhaled a long, slow breath. "No. It's too dangerous. Too many deaths."

Dal leaned back in his seat and raised his hairy eyebrows like when he had a winning move at chess. "And staying here isn't?"

James considered the impending attack of moonshiners coupled with the plan to nuke them all. Even if his group survived the mob and stocked their shelves high, did they really want to huddle underground for the rest of their lives, hoping rations wouldn't run out? "You've got me there."

"Exactly." Dal slumped forward, clicking off the screens as if in resignation.

James's mind whirled with all the possibilities and probable outcomes. "Even if we secure this quasi-built ship, who's going to fly it?"

The room had gone black, and only their haloed heads illuminated their faces. Dal folded his hands on the table as if further discussion was unnecessary. "You."

"You're kidding me. I've never flown anything that large."

Dal grinned. "Practice makes perfect."

James's wristband beeped. He glanced down at the time and his stomach sunk. "Dammit, Dal, the *Expedition* is leaving in fifteen minutes."

Dal gave him a knowing twitch of his eyebrow. "Do you *really* want to see it take off?"

"I have to." James shot toward the door, adjusting his backpack.

"Whatever you do, don't try to defend the governor. Leave that to her bodyguards. They view all gangs as threats, and you'd be killed along with the Razornecks."

"I won't." Although the governor had always been a

thorn in his side, James still worried about her and her family surviving the attack. Yes, she blew up Utopia and planned to abandon her own city, but she didn't deserve to be taken out by the Razornecks. Besides, James needed some sort of structure until the *Expedition* took off and he could get to the *Destiny*. If the Razornecks gained control of the city, every street would go to hell. He pressed the panel and the sides parted, revealing a crowded corridor.

"James, you never agreed to fly the *Destiny*." Dal's voice was a gripping force, holding him back.

James turned around. "You know me better than that, Dal. You know it's a yes."

Dal's face softened. "All the more reason to be careful. We can't have the most important person in the Radioactive Hand disappearing on us. Every time you go through those passages, you risk your life."

James shot Dal a steady stare. "I'll be back. Besides, some things are worth the risk."

Chapter Two

Fireworks

"Don't go." Skye sunk into the recycled plastic couch. Her hopes wheezed out of her lungs like the air from the ripped cushions.

Grease shook his head in a jerking motion. His fingers twitched as he paced their small apartment collecting knives, scissors, anything sharp. The desperation teeming in his wild eyes pushed Skye to the edge of giving up.

But not quite. "Why aren't Carly and I enough?"

"The bombing of Utopia killed a lot of Razornecks. With that hard-nosed witch in charge, we can't get anything for ourselves. You have to look at the big picture. We could have all the food we need. Think of Carly."

"Carly, my ass," Skye whispered, hoping the child still napped in the other room. Anger simmered in her chest. Only a slime would blame this risky escapade on a little girl. "I see the bigger picture, all right."

The plastic crinkled as she shot up and grabbed his arm. Grease fought her, twisting away from her grip in a weak tug.

Her fingernails dug into his skin as she turned his arm over to the pale underside. Puncture marks ran in a line from his wrist to his elbow. Black circles spread like blood underneath his skin around each mark.

"This isn't just about revenge. It's that crap from the moon, isn't it?"

His arm slipped from her fingers as his eyes flicked down, the dilated pupils shifty. "It's not just for that. The Razornecks need control of the city. They want to make the rations fair."

She put her hands on her hips and squeezed her sides. "And have a steady shipment of moonshine in return?"

He didn't argue her point. "Taking out Governor Grier is the only way."

"Besides being murder, it's too dangerous. You saw what they did to Utopia. I almost died from worry when you came home so late. I thought the blast killed you."

He smoothed his hand over the metal ridges on the back of his neck, implanted when he became a member of the gang. The enhancements used to excite her, but now they stirred up animosity for the people ruining Grease's life.

"The Razornecks aren't going to let that happen. Not again." He sounded nervous, as if he didn't believe it himself. "Besides, somethin's going on with those green-haired idealists of the Radioactive Hand. They usually don't let us get ahead, but they've removed most of their patrols."

"If they have, there's a reason for it. Think, Grease. Why would they be drawing back?"

Grease shrugged, his shoulder bones protruding from underneath his ripped T-shirt. "Who cares? It allows us to steal what we deserve."

Anger hardened inside her, twisting her stomach muscles. "You think you're indestructible, that moonshine gives you powers no one else can beat, but it takes away life as well.

Look at you. You're turning into a shell of a man, following crazy orders, pumping alien substances into your veins, twitching like you can't keep still."

He winced, pulling away from her like a wounded jackal. Guilt seeped into her broken heart, but she couldn't let him get away with another heist. Each time he left, the Razornecks raised the stakes. At first, all they wanted was fair food rations, but ever since they got into Morpheus, they coveted power.

"Please, Grease. Think about your daughter. What would the two of us do without you?"

"I'm coming back." He zipped up his backpack and threw it over his shoulder. "When I do, you'd better be here."

She leaned in, smelling the pungent odor of rotting orchids. He used to smell like sweat and cigarettes, normal things. "Only if you give up that moon-crack."

He gawked at her as if she'd asked him to give up breathing. "Not gonna happen, Skye."

Hopelessness spun a black hole in her stomach and she dropped to her knees. "I've heard horrible rumors. City guardians talk of changed people outside the gates, people who took the drug for so long it ate away their soul. What if you turn into one of those moonshiners?"

"Scare tactics." He kicked the door open and the musty smell of the old hall carpet wafted in. "Made up to keep the lower class in line. They're afraid of us. Believe me, I'll know when to stop."

"Please." She gulped back a sob, realizing she feared him as well. The man who had saved her was slipping through her fingers, and she was helpless to save him in return. Where was the resourcefulness she'd had all those years on the streets? She felt useless and weak, unable to seize fate in her hands and turn it around. She had failed him.

"Watch for me on the holoscreen." He saluted her with a

goofy wave of his hand over his eyebrow, and for a moment, the old Grease flashed before her, the man who had found her pillaging in the alleys and given her a home.

"Tell Carly her dad's a hero." Grease turned and disappeared around the corner.

Skye stumbled after him but crumpled against the doorframe. She couldn't leave Carly alone, and she had already given everything she had to convince him not to go. When Grease made a decision, he stuck to it.

Her heart squeezed, and she took deep breaths to calm down. She couldn't shake the feeling this whole mission would fail. The Razornecks had never attempted such a bold attack on government soil.

"Where's Daddy, Skye?"

Skye whirled around. Carly stood in the kitchen, rubbing her fist against her eye. One-legged Jennifer dangled from underneath her arm, the doll half dressed in rags. Blond hair stuck up from Carly's ponytail, which had shifted to the right side of her head.

Skye didn't want to upset her, but she didn't want to lie, either. "He's gone to work, Carls."

"When will he be back?"

She avoided Carly's eyes as she closed the door and fumbled with a dishcloth, wrapping it around a hook on the wall. In her opinion, he wasn't coming back. "I don't know."

"I miss him." Carly hugged Jennifer closer, and the doll's innocent eyes stared at Skye. She should have tried harder to convince him to stay.

"I know. I do, too."

The holoscreen tempted Skye from their family room, the long crack down the middle glistening in the yellowish, fluorescent overhead light. She couldn't watch the news team covering the assassination, especially with Carly awake.

Anxiety rippled inside her and the walls of their small apartment felt like they were pressing in. She had to see the State Building for herself, to be there when the attack struck. The wallscreen would show footage close up, and she didn't want her seeing the violence firsthand, but from the roof she could at least guess who was winning.

She took Carly's hand. "Come on. Let's get you dressed. We're going to the upper levels."

"That's our last pass. You said not until an emergency—"

"I know what I said." Leading her to the family room, Skye dug in a pile of old clothes Grease had pilfered and found a tattered pink coat Carly's size. She shoved the thermal stuffing back in the ripped arm and pulled it over the little girl's pajamas. "We have to go."

"*Beach Party Rules* is on in an hour," Carly whined and pulled on Jennifer's hair.

Skye gave her a stern look. Even though she wasn't her biological mom, she knew what was good for her and what wasn't. "You shouldn't be watching that junk, anyway."

They hurried down the dimly lit hall to the stairway at the back. Gangs had shattered most of the bulbs into razor-bladed flower petals. The lights still intact flickered in and out.

"Just a few floors until the elevators work, Carls. We can do it."

Grease had promised them a spot on Level Twenty-Two someday, but she knew his assurance was nothing more than a pipe dream. By the time they reached the fourth floor, Carly was dragging her feet.

"I'm tired."

Skye wanted to lecture her about how, at six years old, she was a big girl who could walk on her own, but there wasn't enough time to argue. The attack could happen at any minute.

"Come on, I'll carry you the rest of the way."

She picked up Carly, and the girl wrapped her arms around Skye's neck.

Skye leaped up the next few flights, taking two steps at a time. When she reached the eighteenth level, her heart was hammering against her chest. She'd lost some of her steam from her alley days, sitting on that sticky couch, waiting for her life to improve and doing a whole lot of nothing to fix it.

Well, I'm doing something now.

"It's too bumpy; slow down." Carly buried her face in Skye's shoulder.

"I can't. We've got to keep going. We're almost there."

She passed a landing covered in old soybean wrappers and damaged electronics. She knew Carly would love more wires to braid, but she couldn't stop now. The numbers painted on the wall read LEVEL TWENTY. Goose bumps prickled her skin. She'd only come up this high once before.

Two armed men stood at the top of the stairwell, holding gallium lasers on either side, equipped with enough voltage to kill an elephant, if one still existed. Their faces were set in grim lines that warned, *Don't even try.*

The man on the right, dressed in an old military uniform with a gray buzz cut, held out his hand and wiggled his fingers impatiently. The other guard stared at her as though he'd be surprised if she could form coherent sentences, never mind give a valid reason to cross. "Upper Level Pass."

Still holding Carly, Skye jammed her free hand into her pocket and dug out two plastic cards, hoping the guards wouldn't track them back to their original owners. Grease had given her four passes after coming home late one night, telling her not to ask questions. Skye had used the first two to take Carly to a licensed doctor when she had a bad fever and had saved these last two ever since.

The man narrowed his eyes, smoothing his thumb over

the barcode. "Purpose?"

"Private visitation."

He sniffed as though anyone she'd visit would live on the levels below. Looking down at her yellow-stained T-shirt and torn jeans, Skye suddenly felt self-conscious.

"All right." The cards disappeared into his front pocket, and Skye's stomach lurched as if he'd kept her left arm. Had she made the right decision? Would she need the passes in the future?

"Give me your hands."

She held out a palm, and Carly followed her example. The guard ran a scanner over their skin, and a series of blue numbers appeared on their wrists. Skye smoothed her fingers over hers, seeing her favorite number five in the middle. Perhaps it was a good sign.

"Expires in twenty-four hours."

"Yes, sir." She checked the holoscreen above their heads and noted the time.

He grunted. "You and the girl may pass."

As the guards moved aside, Skye slipped into a corridor with bright, fluorescent lights and a plush carpet that crushed under her feet, releasing the smell of lilacs. Soft, synthesized tones floated into her ears. Ignoring the vases of plastic hyacinths and the holopaintings shimmering on the walls, she reached a working elevator with a panel lit in green light. She placed Carly down, pressed the panel, and stretched her sore arms.

The elevator door slid away and they stepped in. The floor surged underneath their feet and Carly's eyes widened.

Skye grabbed her hand, anxious to reach the roof before it was too late.

Not that I can do anything to change the outcome. I'll just be staring like a puppet with no strings.

Carly put her other hand on the floor, her moist fingers making halos of condensation on the chrome.

The elevator beeped and they stepped onto a cement walkway with greenhouses stacked in rows. The sky opened in an infinite ceiling above their heads and the sun blazed, brighter than any light they'd ever seen. Carly jumped out. "Cyber beans!"

"Be careful." Skye noticed Carly's pale arms, white as bone. "Pull your sleeves down and don't take off your coat."

She took the girl's hand and they weaved through the greenhouses. A heavy security system armed each structure, lasers glowing neon blue across the glass doors. The plants looked so withered and fragile; Skye wondered how they could produce any food at all. Especially with Utopia gone, the rations would get even smaller.

"Can I go inside and touch the plants?"

"No, Carls. I'm sorry. The buildings are locked."

They reached the edge of the rooftop with a panoramic view across the New York skyline. Blocks of high-rises cluttered the horizon like a jar of pencils all sticking up. It appeared city planners heaped each building next to the other, so close she could jump from one to another. On the right, smoke plumed from the broken glass of Utopia. Architects and bioengineers designed the structure to catch and magnify the sun's rays for five levels of accelerated growth. The single building produced more food than all the others in the city combined.

Skye avoided looking over there, not wanting to see the devastation. In the center of the city, a tower topped with a golden dome structure stood out like a crystal.

The State Building. Home of the richest woman in the city. The woman Grease wanted dead.

Her stomach sickened as she thought of him working his

way through the underground and emerging at the top of the State Building's marble stairs with the rest of the Razornecks carrying armfuls of lasers and knives. The building looked so serene and impenetrable. Didn't the governor have a family? Children of her own around Carly's age?

Collapsing against the side of a greenhouse, Skye didn't want him to succeed. If the Razornecks gained control of the city, they'd have endless food and power. She and Carly would never go hungry again. But would it be right to take out the people in charge? Starve the rest of the city? Give the Razornecks unlimited amounts of a drug that would turn them violent against civilians?

All I want is for Grease to come home.

She sighed, watching Carly play with a beetle as it scurried around real grass growing at the base of the greenhouse. She wished she could give her so much more than a one-day field trip to a dwindling food resource.

Eruptions boomed, echoing between the buildings, making it difficult for Skye to discern the source. She scrambled to her feet and leaned against the railing. Her fingers shook as she gripped the rusty rail.

Carly ran up beside her and grabbed onto her arm. "What was that?"

"Bombs." She hadn't seen Grease take anything explosive with him, but that didn't mean the other members of the gang didn't carry hypergrenades. Laser fire pinged through the alleyways, echoing over the city. Grease wasn't kidding around. The battle had begun.

A cloud shielded the sun, and the roof darkened. Skye shivered in the absence of the warm rays, wishing she'd taken another minute to dig out a coat for herself. She wasn't accustomed to the rush of raw wind on her skin.

Carly tugged on her arm. "I want to go back. I don't like

it up here."

"The sun will break through again." Skye tried to sound reassuring, but her voice broke on the words.

Grease may not. He already tried his luck once.

Behind them, the sky rumbled like thunder. She spun around as five large military hovercrafts sped over their heads. Carly ducked, holding her hands to her ears.

One word came to Skye's mouth and sat on her tongue, unable to be spoken.

No.

Her words from their fight came back to her. *You saw what they did to Utopia.*

What if it was a trap, meant to catch the remaining gang members? Her stomach pitched. Missiles, swelling as large as whales, clung to both sides of the hovercrafts.

Skye's fingers gripped the railing so hard the rust cut into her skin. Carly hugged her leg, unable to stand. The hovercrafts glided to the golden dome and surrounded the perimeter. Skye strained her ears, but she couldn't hear anything above the engines' roar.

Would the government destroy the one building that kept the city unified? Maybe the pilots were bluffing. She dug her toes into the bottom of her sneakers and hoped.

An eternity passed with the ships hovering like giant wasps. She should have tied Grease to the couch or hit his head hard enough to knock him out. She breathed in guilt like air, and it spread through her body, making her fingers shake. She didn't have the gumption. Her problem in life had always been inaction, and now she had paid for it.

Other spectators cluttered the buildings around them, everyone staring at the last pillar of civilization, hoping the same thing she did.

Don't blow it up.

One of the hovercrafts parked on a loading dock toward the top of the government building. Skye squinted to see farther, wishing she'd found a decent pair of glasses in her scrounging days. It looked as though a few people were running from the ramp to board it. Had the governor gotten away? The hovercraft rose to the sky and flew off.

In unison, the other hovercrafts backed up, and relief tingled through Skye like rain on her skin. She gasped in and held her breath, waiting for them to withdraw and fly away as well.

Suddenly, the hovercrafts fired in unison, twin sets of missiles from each vessel plunging into the golden dome. The building shattered and collapsed inward. Flames sparked from the center, and black smoke rose to congeal with the smog in the sky.

Skye's knees weakened, and she collapsed to the ground.

"Grease!" She shouted his name repeatedly at the burning inferno until her voice gave out. Uncontrollable sobs wracked her body. She hugged Carly tightly, shielding the little girl's eyes from the searing smoke blowing in their direction. Without him, she was all the girl had. That wasn't very much.

"Was Daddy in there?"

Skye looked away. Her eyes stared at the horizon, but she couldn't focus on anything. She lacked the courage to reply.

Chapter Three

Meteor

James raced through the grimy blackness of the subway, checking his wristband every five seconds and cursing the unforgiving tick of time.

Just wait until a moonshiner gets in my way now.

He ran with his laser ready to fire, and knew exactly where to aim. Every step brought back another memory: the first time he saw Mestasis crouched behind machinery, holding a small kitten. Her skin shone so dark she blended in with the shadows. The whites of her eyes had given her away, bright as the moon before the mining began. Bright and hopeful, not like anything else ever gracing the lower levels. He remembered their first kiss in the coffee shop, an electric charge sweeping through him, making everyone else disappear. And he remembered the lights breaking into shards with her powers, scaring away Razornecks so they could escape.

He'd saved her life, and she'd saved his in return. A bond thicker than anything he could ever imagine. She was special, and he hated how he had to use her abilities to help his people, to further his own cause. It was only when his cause became her own, and he realized she'd be safer on that ship than on Earth, that he allowed destiny to take its course, a course that would ultimately usher her away from him.

He emerged into the smog of day and peered up to see if the Expedition had taken off, but the pollution was too thick to spot anything in the sky. He jumped into the nearest open window and climbed until the stairs took him to the first working elevator. At this point, he didn't dare look at the time.

The elevator couldn't move quickly enough for him. He pressed her floor and watched as the numbers accumulated and he entered the levels for the New York branch of the Telepathic Institute of New England, or TINE. Usually the doors were heavily guarded, but Mestasis had won seats on the *Expedition* for everyone at TINE, so the corridor leading to her room was as silent as a city after a nuke attack.

The door to her room lay open, and he ran in shouting her name. All cabinets, all walls were stripped bare. He ran to the room where he'd woken up that morning. Empty.

He ran his hands over the silken sheets. A black hole formed in his chest, sucking his breath away. Mestasis was gone. Maybe it was better he'd left when he did, because he wasn't sure he could have let her go if he had the chance again.

An explosion pounded in his gut, shaking the walls around him. Was it the assassination attempt, or had the *Expedition* just take off?

James ran to the elevator and slammed the roof button over and over until his palm hurt. The panel beeped and the doors parted. A female voice chimed: *You've reached level seventy-eight.*

TINE's building wasn't the tallest skyscraper in New York, but it was high enough to break through the smog. Smoke blackened the sky in the north end, the plumes spreading like a mushroom cloud over the city. *The attack must have happened hours ago.* Which meant he'd heard the engines of the *Expedition.* Sure enough, an orange and gray streak stained the sky above the pluming black clouds. James ran along the length of the roof, shouting Mestasis's name.

The ship resembled a reverse meteor, rising from the horizon into the russet-stained sky. Meteors destroyed life, but this flaming ball carried life with it. Thousands of people rode to a paradise planet, transporting the hope of a renewed civilization. James watched the arc with steady eyes, reluctant to look away.

Mestasis.

He whispered her name like a prayer uttered before sleep. His heart ached and he wondered if it would stop beating altogether as the chord binding their souls stretched farther and farther apart.

I'll never see her again.

The finality of the thought filled him with dread, yet he knew he'd made the best decision for both of them. Of all his concerns, the most prevalent was her safety, and she would live longer and more comfortably on that ship than anyone here on Earth.

His finger rose to the sky, tracing the arc to touch the *Expedition* one last time. The ship had grown so small; he could cover it with the tip of his finger, the finger that had trailed circles on her neck only hours ago.

It's best this way.

If Thadious Legacy's DNA tests had granted James a ticket, he'd never have been able to live with himself, knowing he left everyone "not deemed suitable" behind to die on a planet with a one-way ticket to hell. He shouldn't have grown so attached to Mestasis, but she'd caught him off guard from the first day he saw her in the lower levels, wearing her pristine uniform of the Telepathic Institute of New England, risking everything to save the life of a kitten.

If I'd made it on the ship, would we have married?

Another second passed, and the glinting silver speck winked out. Ignoring the hole aching inside him, James pulled himself up, collected his backpack, and descended to the lower levels. Night—or what was left of it—approached quickly. Thanks to Mestasis, he had secured three hundred of his people a place aboard that ship.

Now he needed to tend to the rest.

Chapter Four

Break In

Carly shook a box of soycaroni. "I'm hungry."

"Go back to your room." Half hearing her, Skye crouched on the floor of the apartment, hugging her knees with both arms. Footage of the assassination attempt flashed on the wall, replaying over and over like a movie with a bad ending.

The newscaster, a young man with a crew cut and a perfect dent in his chin, spoke with a careless, monotone voice. "Although Governor Grier survived the attack, her two children and her husband are still missing. Several members of the Razorneck gang are credited with the assassination attempt, and"—he actually smiled—"I'm hearing reports that none, I repeat, none of the gang members survived."

Razornecks lay dead from burns or laser wounds. Fire crews struggled to control the blazing heaps of desks and broken wallscreens, and newscasters shouted over the hissing flames. So much death, and no sign of Grease.

"Don't worry, Skye. Daddy got away," Carly said.

That got her attention.

Skye tore her gaze from the holoscreen. Carly stood sucking on a large plastic spoon. She sounded so certain. Was it denial?

Skye sighed, taking the box from her. "Okay, I'll make dinner." How could she tell her that if Grease hadn't come home by now, he must be dead? The government wasn't taking prisoners.

But the world had to go on. Dinner needed to be made. It was about time she got up and faced reality. Skye left the screen on and dragged herself into the kitchen. She pressed the panel on the stove and the burner heated up.

An expiration date six months past was stamped on the back of the box. She opened the cabinets and found a few soy wafers, old rice patties, and a bottle of gelatinous ketchup. Why couldn't Grease bring home more food and less moonshine?

Figuring expired soycaroni was better than nothing, Skye filled a pot with water, making sure to use only enough to soften the soycaroni, and watched it rumble to a boil. Soon she'd have to search for food the only way she knew how: pilfering the garbage heaps in the alleys every morning when the higher-ups threw down what they didn't want. The thought of it made the soycaroni seem like five-star-restaurant fare.

The holoscreen flickered from the other room, and Skye wondered if it had dimmed forever. She had found it in a recycling chute a year back, so any picture they received was a miracle.

After stirring the water, she ducked into the living room. A primly dressed reporter with blond bombshell curls and wearing a pink pencil skirt spoke into a microphone in the darkness. A rusty subway train loomed behind her.

What would a high-rise person be doing in the underground? Skye had never even gone down *that* far.

"We interrupt this program to bring you a breaking

newscast. Crazed vagrants believed to be moonshiners have broken into the city using the old sewage drainpipes. They're crawling up to the lower levels and attacking anyone who gets in their way. Recovering after the assassination attempt on her life, Governor Grier has issued an advisory asking everyone on Levels One through Twenty to stay in their homes and lock their doors."

Skye froze, watching as the camera turned to guards with gallium lasers blasting a darting shadow in the distance. It moved too fast to be a normal person, careering off walls like a monkey, and Skye wondered if the stories she'd heard about the moonshiners were true.

"The water's boiling!" Carly's voice startled her, and she whipped around, feeling as though she were stuck in some nightmare and would soon wake up beside Grease's ruddy face, safe and protected.

Skye scrambled over to the empty food cabinet. She braced herself against the frame and started to push. The cabinet creaked as it moved, revealing a pile of dust and rat excrement underneath.

Carly yelled behind her, "What about the soycaroni? What are you doing?"

"Keeping us safe." She shoved the cabinet directly against the front door. If Grease came back, he wouldn't be able to get in, but after seeing that man on TV fly through the sewers, she couldn't take a chance.

"Carly, help me find more things to pile against the door." The couch was too big for her to lift, but the mattresses on the floor would add more weight behind the barricade. She ran into the family room. Pillows fell as she picked up the mattress they all slept on.

Carly threw everything she could lift against the door, including Jennifer. The doll hit the plastic and slumped down on the floor. "Is that good?"

"Yes, Carls. Great job. Jennifer can be the lookout." The heat rose in their tiny apartment. Skye swiped sweat off her forehead, realizing she'd left the water boiling. Returning to the stove, she tore open the box and poured in the soycaroni. The routine of watching the geometric shapes turn in the water made the situation feel normal again, and she breathed a sigh of relief.

Maybe she'd overreacted. The newscasters always seemed to make more out of a single incident. Their apartment was on the third floor, levels up from the tunnels.

"I'm sorry I scared you." She gestured for the girl to come closer. "You know I get jumpy with your daddy not around."

"It's okay." Just as Carly came over and wrapped her arms around Skye's waist, a scream rose up from the lower levels outside their balcony.

Skye picked up Carly and hurried out the back door, then peered over the balcony railing. A blur of movement scurried down the alley, throwing up trash. A can scuttled against the building, sending a pigeon flapping into the air. Two people dashed from the window underneath them to the adjacent building.

"Are those the people they were talking about on TV?" Carly's fingers tightened around Skye's neck.

"Probably just scavengers or gang members." Skye leaned over to get a better look, but the alley rats had disappeared.

Light, cruel laughter wafted up, the sound reminding Skye of an upper-level heiress teasing her servant. An arm darted out of a lower window and squirmed as if feeling around for a way out. The arm twitched and bent backward, making Skye's stomach tighten. Dirty fingers grabbed a piece of trash, and then disappeared back inside. A woman shouted from another level, and Skye heard the pulsing sound of lasers echo against the buildings.

"Come on. Let's go back inside." She'd seen enough to know they should lay low. Pulling the balcony door closed, she locked it with the dead bolt.

The reek of burned soycaroni filled the apartment, and Skye plopped Carly down on the couch and rushed to the stove. The water had evaporated and the soycaroni solidified against the bottom, turning to blackened sludge.

"Dammit." Skye had wasted their only box of food.

That was the least of their problems, though. She stiffened as she realized black smoke was leaking out the crack in the top of the front door.

"No, no, no." Skye fanned the smoke and reopened the balcony door. She grabbed the pot handle and burned her fingers, whipping back her hand.

"Be careful!" Carly stood on the couch watching what Skye was doing.

"I *am* being careful." She slipped her hand into a ripped oven glove and carried the pot to the balcony, throwing it over the ledge to the garbage below.

"That was our dinner!" Carly wailed.

She didn't have time to answer. Something thumped against the front door, rattling the cabinet and knocking the mattress down. Dust plumed from the crack between the door and the floor. Skye froze, fear eating away at her composure. *This can't be happening.*

Another thump. The plastic door cracked under the weight.

Carly screamed.

The cabinet wouldn't hold the door in place for long. Skye dug around the piles of junk, searching for weapons, but Grease had taken them all with him.

Selfish bastard. Anger spread through her. Not only had

Grease taken their only chance to defend themselves, he'd left them utterly alone. Skye trembled as she realized she was the only person she could be truly angry with. She'd let him go.

I could use those passes now.

Backing up to the family room, she took Carly's hand and led her out onto the balcony. The cabinet crashed to the floor as she pulled the balcony's glass door closed in front of the girl. Carly's horrified look made Skye's heart clamp. She mouthed, "Stay there," and searched for anything she could find to fend off the intruder. As something rattled in the kitchen, Skye dug through the heaps of garbage in the living room. That pot would have come in handy right now. As she pulled up rags and broken plastic containers, she vowed to be cleverer. How else would she ever be a good mother?

A strange keening noise rose from the other room and an old woman wearing a pale floral skirt and a yellow apron came around the corner. Her hair was neatly tied in a bun, but thick, black veins protruded from her arms and legs like worms. And her eyes didn't seem right—a little too big and too slanted, almost almond-shaped. Those eyes zeroed in on Skye and a wicked grin showed black, pointed teeth.

What's wrong with this lady? Is she a moonshiner?

The woman moved much too quickly for her age, pushing against the walls as she scrambled toward Skye. Skye backed up against the wallscreen. The pretty reporter hovered over her left shoulder, now talking about a soap ad.

This is it. Find something to throw or you're dead.

Skye whirled around and pulled the wallscreen out of its mount, wires sizzling as they detached. She threw it at the old woman, and the moonshiner flew back against the wall under its weight.

Only her black veined legs stuck out from under the broken screen, twitching with pumping blood. Skye breathed a sigh of relief, trying not to look. She moved toward the balcony when the screen moved and the woman stood up, teeth gnashing together as her broken bones popped back into place.

Skye had heard enough about moonshiners to know she wouldn't win in a hand-to-hand fight. Morpheus made them too fast, and it was hard to kill something already believed to be dead.

Skye lunged for the balcony, swung the glass door open, and shut it behind her. The old woman pushed up against the glass. Her black tongue left a streak of condensation. Skye pushed Carly back. "Don't make a sound."

Tears ran down Carly's cheeks, but the little girl had enough sense to remain silent.

"We'll wait here and maybe she'll go away," Skye whispered in her ear. Although it didn't look like that old woman would go anywhere with them as a lure.

Carly nodded, and her bravery impressed Skye. *If a little girl can hold up, so can I.* They moved to the corner of the balcony and crouched low, holding onto each other.

"What if she doesn't go away?" Carly whispered. "What if she finds a way to unlock the door?"

"Then I'll fight her off as you run back inside."

Carly sniffed and let out a pitiful sob. "But, you'll die."

Skye swallowed, feeling like this was the end of the road. What would Carly do without her? She had no one else. Skye was her guardian now.

The glass door shattered as the armrest of the couch poked through. A hissing laugh wheezed from inside.

Skye scrambled behind it with Carly. They had nowhere to go. Level Three was too high to jump.

"Get on my back. Wrap your arms around my neck and hold on. Really tightly."

Carly piggybacked on top of her, and Skye climbed over the railing. She lowered them, her legs dangling as she grasped the metal poles in her fingers.

In one blink, the woman stood on the armrest like a vulture perched on a branch. Her hair had been pulled from her bun, the gray wisps blowing in the wind. Her face turned in their direction as she searched the horizon with impossibly long eyes that reminded Skye of giant black beetles.

Skye knew if the moonshiner spotted them, she have no choice but to take their chances and let go.

Chapter Five

Chosen One

"You're going to teach me how to fly a star-liner, a deep space colony ship as big as a city with a *video game*?" James leaned over Dal's shoulder as the old man brought up on his miniscreen what looked like a flight simulator program.

"We've tweaked the parameters to correspond to the *Destiny*'s maneuvering capabilities. You fly hovercrafts all the time, right?"

"When I can get my hands on one, yes."

"Flying is flying." Dal handed him the screen. "Make sure you take a look at it."

James clicked off the monitor to save the energy cell and stuck it in his backpack. They walked to the concrete door, passing by guards on either side. "Right. I'll play it while I fight off the moonshiners."

Dal's voice hardened. "Flying's not the hard part."

James stopped and turned toward him. "What *is* the hard part?"

The old man pursed his lips. "Getting to it."

Son of a Razorneck! James realized he'd accepted the mission without even asking about the *Destiny*'s coordinates. That was typical James—he ignored the odds. That's why the Radioactive Hand of Justice promoted him in the first place.

"Where is the *Destiny*?"

Dal scratched his head. "Outside the city, in the Barren Lands on a secret government base called Project Exodus. I've input the coordinates onto the miniscreen."

The mission sounded more and more unattainable, but James stifled his doubt. They had no other choice. "Wow. Getting to the top of the high-rises is one thing, but getting out of the city?"

"You'll have to steal a hovercraft." Dal said it as if he suggested James lift a damaged holoscreen from a Dumpster.

"With the moonshiners breaking in, I don't think there'll be one left to take."

"Try Thadious Legacy's tower." Dal tapped his shoulder. "The man has enough money to own ten of them in all the colors of the rainbow. And I don't think he needs any where he's going."

Dal was right. Thadious's tower was probably empty and unguarded, and no one except the people on that ship, Dal, and James would know. At least they had a plan.

James nodded to one of the guards, a young man with purple-black crescents under his eyes. For a moment, James wondered why he hadn't made it onboard the *Expedition*. Did he choose to stay? Or was he rejected because of some singular strand of his DNA that held a recessive disease?

No matter; James was his only hope now. That thought placed a burden on his shoulders, but it was a burden he was used to. Besides Dal, he was responsible for his gang.

The concrete rolled back, and men pointed lasers into the darkness.

James peered out, and his hair glowed into the shadows, revealing an empty tunnel. He turned back to Dal. "Prepare yourself in case I don't make it back. This mission is almost impossible."

Dal smiled, surprising him. "That's why I asked you to do it."

• • •

James hurried through the old subway tunnel to the stairs leading to the upper levels. Reluctance vibrated through every bone in his body, yet he propelled himself forward like a seeker missile. To visit Thadious Legacy's building would reopen memories he wanted to keep stashed away. He had taken Mestasis there for her interview with the credit hound, and she'd secured the deal allowing James's people on board the *Expedition*. Of course, she thought he'd be invited as well. Fate didn't always work the way you expected.

He tried not to remember how she'd kissed him after the meeting, or the promise of a life together that rested in her dark eyes.

Movement stirred in the alley as he reached the top of the stairway. James fell back into the shadows to pull on his black cap, hiding his glowing hair. His association with his gang was best kept secret. A moonshiner scurried back and forth in a blur of movement. The man stopped every few seconds to crane his neck at an impossible angle toward the upper levels.

James considered sneaking back down and reemerging at the next stop, until he followed the man's gaze to a balcony not too far up. A woman and young girl hung from a railing, legs dangling. An elderly woman with overly large, darkened eyes perched on the balcony railing, wearing a yellow apron and floral skirt. The moonshiner woman flitted from side to side, sniffing the air as if trying to figure out why it smelled like ripe humans.

James brought out his laser, but the man on the ground ran too quickly for him to lock on any target. James fired into the blur to get his attention. Black eyes stared in his direction as the man froze and zeroed in. James started firing, hoping he'd get at least one clean shot in the seconds before the moonshiner reached him.

The man sprinted so quickly, his shoes skimmed the alley and kicked up empty energy cells, the plastic tubes ricocheting off the building. James ducked as the man leaped toward him, his finger never leaving the trigger. White light shot out in a stream as the moonshiner flew through the air with outstretched arms, palms opening and closing. James hit the moonshiner's shoulder, and the force of the laser fire threw him back against the building into a heap of old rags. Before he could recover, James targeted his head. The man hit the building and slumped forward.

James searched the rows of balconies, fearing the woman's grip had slipped, but she hung quietly underneath the old woman's radar. With the weight of the child on her back, she didn't seem to have the strength to hold on much longer. James shot at the balcony, but three floors up was too far to hit anything that moved almost as fast as light. The old woman jumped, skirts flying up around her torso as she plunged to the alley floor after him.

James watched with morbid wonder. *Surely she couldn't survive that fall.*

She landed in a heap of old mattresses and sprang up, flying toward him like a demon.

He fired, feeling as though he was moving in slow motion in a fast-forward world. She crashed into him, and they flew back into a trash heap.

This time, he made a point to hold onto his laser.

He climbed over old boxes and tattered clothes. The woman squirmed above him, biting anything in her way, but she'd lost him in the mess. He fired and she stilled, hanging over a shattered wallscreen. A locket hung from her neck, showing a holopicture of an old man's face. James closed the locket and placed it in the hollow of her neck.

Rest in peace.

Wondering why an old woman would bother with moonshine, James pushed his way up through the garbage. He shouted at the woman and child hanging from the balcony. "Hold on; I'm coming."

James dug in his backpack and pulled out a retractable cable rope. He fired the hook up along the side of the building. The three prongs landed on the balcony floor of the woman's level and he dragged it forward until it caught the railing. Yanking to make sure he'd secured the hook, James fastened the end of the cable rope to his belt and held on as it retracted, pulling him up.

As he rose, he saw the pair in detail. The woman looked to be in her early twenties, startlingly beautiful with curly Irish-red hair and fox-like features. The girl had blond hair and dark eyes, with a cute mushroom-shaped nose and chubby cheeks. He climbed over the railing and offered his hand.

"I'll pull you up."

Her jade eyes flashed him a wary glance before she grasped his arm. He gripped and heaved, lifting her and the little girl over the railing. After wrapping his arms around them, he carried the pair to the end of the couch sticking halfway out the door. One look at the shards of glass told him the moonshiner had put it there.

"Are you okay?"

Shock shone in their wide, blank eyes. He tried the

question again, and the woman nodded, hugging the little girl close.

"How long did you hang out there?"

She croaked, "Too long."

Stepping inside the apartment, he scanned the countertops. A smudged plastic cup lay on its side, a crack running across the bottom. He picked up the cup and tried the faucet to see if they still had water rations. A light stream trickled out. He filled the fake glass until the water petered off and brought it to the balcony, offering it to the woman.

The cup shook in her hands as she sipped. He wanted to bend down and hold it steady for her, but he didn't want to seem too forward, so he stood back and allowed her room to recover.

She offered the girl a drink and glanced up at him. "Thank you."

He waved away her gratitude. "No problem."

"I mean it." A fierce fire simmered in her emerald eyes. She looked like someone out of the old Celtic fairy tales the nurses in the orphanage used to tell him at bedtime. He couldn't imagine why any colony ship would want to leave her DNA behind.

"Thank you for saving us."

"You don't have to thank me. It's what I do."

He contemplated taking them down to the hideout, but he had to press on. The city would be a target soon, and he had to reach the *Destiny* before the world leaders considered it a contaminated zone.

"I need to hurry. Stay here. Wait for a signal from the sky. I'm bringing a ship to evacuate the city."

He turned to leave, but she caught his arm. For someone with small and dainty fingers, she had the grip of a cobra. "Wait! Take us with you. I can help."

He paused, his arm still in her grip. Could he tell her the truth? A stirring in his gut made him trust her, and the city was falling into ruins around them. Who would she tell? "I'm heading to Thadious Legacy's tower to steal a hovercraft. From there, I'm flying across the Barren Lands to a secret government base to hijack a colony ship. I'm not sure it's any safer than staying here. Besides, how can you help? I have to travel quickly."

"I can't stay here. We have no weapons." She stood up, hands on her hips. "But I can watch for moonshiners. You're gonna need a lookout while you finagle a hovercraft."

James scanned the ruined apartment. The front door to the hallway hung by its hinges. Their level was dangerously close to the sewers and moonshiners could storm in at any time. He only had one laser, and he'd need it where he was going. But he couldn't resist those eyes, full of intensity and spirit. And she was right. Three sets of eyes were better than one.

"All right. Pack your belongings; we may not come back."

"What about Daddy?" The girl spoke for the first time, her little hands wrinkling the woman's shirt.

James raised his eyebrow in question. He didn't want to take some other man's family away from him. What was this woman thinking?

"He's gone, Carls, and we have to keep moving." She stepped near James and whispered under her breath. "He's not coming back." Anger hardened her voice.

The girl sniffled, wiping her nose with her hand.

James suddenly felt like an intruder. He shook his head. "Look, I'm not getting in the middle of a family dispute—"

She kept her tone low so the girl couldn't hear. "He was with the Razornecks when they bombed the State Building. Besides, he was half-gone to that moonshine crap when he left."

"Oh." James's throat tightened as he fought the urge to wince. The Razornecks? What had he gotten himself into? He couldn't possibly shelter the family of one of his enemies. What would she think if she saw his neon hair?

Movement rustled in the alley below. They didn't have much time. He had to make a decision.

Hugging the little girl, the woman gazed at him desperately. "We've got nowhere to go."

He had no time to tell her of his affiliations. Besides, he didn't have the heart to give her any reason to distrust him. He couldn't leave her and the girl alone. If he did, he'd always wonder if they survived.

"Okay. Let's go inside and pack up anything you think you'll need."

She thrust out her hand. "I'm Skye O'Connor."

He took her hand, feeling soft skin and small, feminine fingers. "James. James Wilfred."

"This is Carly."

James bent down to her level and offered her his hand. The girl eyed him suspiciously and buried her head in Skye's shoulder.

He took his hand back, knowing he was just a stranger to her, but feeling rejected all the same.

Skye stood up and offered him a sympathetic smile. "Don't worry. She doesn't trust any strangers. It took her a whole month to say one word to me."

Chapter Six

Family

Skye dragged Carly down the hallway, following James as he kicked in a panel she'd passed by a thousand times and never thought to open herself.

"Where are we going?"

The metal clanged and he smiled as the panel settled. "Shortcut."

She had no choice but to trust him. To stay in that apartment would doom her and Carly both. There wasn't any food, and the moonshiner had busted the door. If one person could do so much damage, she couldn't imagine the destruction caused by an army of those monsters.

Carly pulled on her arm. "I don't wanna go." Her lower lip trembled and Skye bent down to meet her eye to eye.

"It's the only way, Carls."

Besides, she realized she did trust James. He had an innate confidence and meaning about the way he held himself, like he served some greater purpose and had nothing to hide. He also looked like he'd walked right out of a comic book, with a strong-boned face, sleek dark hair, and lean, rounded muscles rippling down to his stomach underneath his tight black shirt.

Trying not to stare as he peered in the hole he'd made, she curbed her hope. What he said about saving people for a living seemed almost too good to be true. Who does that? A superhero?

James signaled them in. "Come on, the coast is clear."

"But what about Daddy?" Carly tugged on Skye's arm.

She couldn't wait for Grease forever. Skye sighed and looked back over her shoulder one more time, feeling a pang of guilt. "I left a note in a secret place only he'd think to look, telling him where we're going, okay Carls? If he comes back, he'll find us."

Carly bit her lip, tucking Jennifer into her coat. "Okay."

Skye wished they could leave the doll. Carrying a nonessential item would only slow Carly down. But a few years back, a man dressed as Santa had come around to their apartment on Christmas and given it to her. It wasn't just a doll—it was a sign that humanity still existed in the small cracks between the Morpheus users.

Ducking into the hole, Skye followed Carly onto a landing platform to a maintenance shaft. A series of metal rungs led to the upper levels. "Carly, you go first. Can you hold on tight?"

"Uh-huh."

"Move one foot at a time, and don't look down."

"What if I fall?" Carly reached up and grabbed the next rung and Skye's heart leapt as her little hand slipped and then clung again.

"I'll catch you."

"But what if you fall, too?"

"I'll catch you both." James spoke up from underneath them. The certainty in his voice must have convinced Carly, because she kept climbing.

They reached Level Twenty within the hour. Skye thought they'd meet laser barrels at the top, but someone had sealed the passage a long time ago, and no one guarded it.

"How did you know about this?"

"Building plans." He clung to another rung beneath them and shot a glance down to see if anyone followed them. "You'd be surprised how many secret passageways architects hid in these high-rises."

If only she'd known. She could have saved those passes in the first place.

James kicked in the panel on Level Twenty, checking to see if anyone was in the hallway. After winking back at her, he led them into the same corridor she'd been granted access to just hours ago. He put his finger to his lips, and they tiptoed to the working elevator. He pressed the panel for Level Fifty-Four.

"We're not going to the top?" she whispered, afraid the guards that had let her through could hear them down the hall.

"No. Level Fifty-Four connects to the recycling factory, which connects to Thadious Legacy's tower."

The elevator beeped, and they stepped in. She felt the platform rise underneath her sneakers and was grateful to leave the lower levels behind. "How are you going to get by the guards?"

"They're not there. No one is. Thadious Legacy left this morning with all of his people on a colony ship called the *Expedition*."

"No way." Skye had only heard rumors. It was strange to think of people abandoning Earth, leaving the rest of them behind.

"It's true. They kept it top secret because they didn't want a horde storming the ship, trying to get on."

"I've heard generations will live their entire lives on the ship."

James nodded, his lips set in a grim line. "That is correct."

"It boggles my mind. What do you think about living your whole life on a ship?"

"I try not to think about it." James's smoky eyes darkened as if he was hardening inside, shutting her out. He looked away, studying the elevator panel as the numbers ascended.

Level Thirty-Seven.

Level Thirty-Eight.

His silence intrigued Skye. She'd touched upon a sensitive subject. "Did you want to be on that ship?"

James winced and turned away. "I couldn't be on it. That's all I'll say."

Couldn't be on it? Skye picked at her fingernail as questions swirled through her head.

Carly made circles in the chrome with her sweaty fingers. She'd drawn a flower and a smiley face. "Are we almost there?"

"Soon, Carls." If she'd wanted to ask James anything further about the *Expedition*, the time had come and gone. Best to drop the subject and allow him to focus on getting them out of the city.

The elevator beeped and a monotone voice announced, "Level Fifty-Four."

The doors parted to a lobby area with live tropical ferns and windows the length of the walls. The moon gleamed through the glass like a pockmarked face, with dark spots where the mining crews had splurged.

James paused. "This isn't supposed to be occupied." People mingled around tables drinking cocktails, and waiters dressed in black suits carried food on trays. Had they forgotten the end of the world? Or were they untouchable?

Skye glanced down at her yellow stained T-shirt. "I can't go out there in this." She felt like a ragamuffin going to a princess's ball.

James took her hand and squeezed. He whispered in her ear, "We don't have time to backtrack. Besides, you look stunning. Just act normal, like we're a real family."

Stunning? Skye's cheeks flamed at the compliment and she looked away, feeling her palm burn against his. He held out a hand for Carly, but the girl scowled and scurried behind her. Skye took her hand instead. "Okay, dear husband, lead us on."

The corner of James's lips curved up at her comment. He directed them behind the majority of the congregation, around a stone fountain. Dolphins leaped above cascading water to glittering rocks in a pool below. Carly moved to grab a tail, but Skye pulled her back.

"Not now." She didn't want them attracting any unnecessary attention.

The trays of food smelled sublime: honey roasted chicken, baked crab, and lemon meringue pie. Skye's stomach murmured and she stifled her raw hunger, trying to remember the last time she had food in her belly. The opulence of the upper levels disgusted her so much, she almost lost her appetite. She glanced over at James and watched him flinch as a waiter passed. Had he the same disdain for the upper class?

"Skye…I'm hungry." Carly tugged her arm to get closer to the silver trays.

"No, absolutely not." She felt like such a prude, but she couldn't explain to Carly how much danger surrounded them. She didn't want to upset her. Besides, they had no cards with credits. She couldn't so much as buy one bite.

"Soon." James flashed his misty eyes at Carly, and she quieted, staying by Skye's side.

A woman in red silk sat on the fountain's edge, watching Carly stare at the dolphins like watching an imp steal a piece of cheese. The woman raised her hand to brush back her wavy, auburn hair, exposing a series of blue numbers on her wrist. Everyone on the upper levels had the barcodes, identifying their status. Hers and Carly's had disappeared in twenty-four hours, like the guard had said. If anyone saw their bare wrists now, they'd thrown them back into the alleys—if they were lucky.

Skye twisted her wrists down to hide the pale, bare skin, feeling ugly, naked, and small among the cultured citizens with their sleek hair, straight white teeth, and tailored clothes. It was like walking into a movie on the wallscreen, where everything and everyone looked picture perfect.

"You're doing great," James whispered in her ear, as if sensing her self-consciousness. "Just a few more steps."

They reached the far side of the room, where a ramp attached their building to the next.

A voice boomed on the intercom. "The *Heritage* will be accepting its first round of passengers in one hour. Everyone with A-group boarding passes may report to the roof immediately."

"Seems we've stumbled upon a farewell party," James whispered as he bowed to another man like he knew him. "Good day, sir."

"And yourself." The man waltzed off with a complacent smile on his face. Skye watched him through the crowd, narrowing her eyes as she heard him compliment the weave of the napkins.

He must be in A-group.

She wondered what it felt like to live the life of the elite, to never freeze in an alley or chew plastic to stave off hunger. Yes, they were beautiful, but they were also soft, their conversations pleasant but meaningless, which made them more vulnerable than she was. For a moment she was proud of her orphan upbringing. It had molded her into a survivor.

And she planned to stay that way.

Just a few more tables separated them from the ramp leading to the adjacent building. Skye glanced over her shoulder, feeling her skin prickle. The woman in the red silk dress spoke with a security guard near the fountain. She stared in their direction, and then turned back to the guard. Skye tensed, trying not to break into a run. She squeezed James's hand and he bowed his head to hear her voice over the conversations in the room.

"I think we've been spotted."

He kept his eyes on the ramp. "We're almost there."

A guard speaking into a mini-mic stood in the middle of the ramp. He gave James a wary look. "Let me see your family's boarding passes, sir."

"We're not going on the ship. I merely came to say goodbye to a friend." James's voice was smooth as velvet, and Skye thought the guard would buy it. She would have.

The guard took one look at the thermal stuffing falling out of Carly's coat. Jennifer's head poked out, the doll's scraggly blond hair falling across Carly's arm. He narrowed his eyes. "Turn over your wrist."

James released Skye's hand gently. "Honey, I think it's time to run."

Skye froze in shock as James's fist arced up and hit the man in the jaw. The security guard went down, but another shouted from the room behind them. "Outsiders!"

"Run!" James repeated, whipping out his laser.

Adrenaline rushing, Skye picked up Carly and sprinted down the ramp. Her sneakers squeaked on the chrome like tiny alarms, and laser fire erupted behind her as James shot to keep the other guards at bay.

She reached the bottom of the ramp and darted to the right, guessing which way to go. Large vats of brown sludge gurgled beneath her feet as she ran across metal grating. The stench of mold and rot wafted up and Carly covered her nose. What were they recycling?

James reached the bottom of the ramp just as she found a connecting balcony that led to the other side. He paused, firing shots around the corner, than followed her down the metal walkway.

"What is this place?" she shouted as they reached the other side and leaped down the stairs two at a time.

"A food recycling facility."

"What's in the vats?

"You don't want to know."

Laser shots fired from the opposite balcony, singeing black marks in the chrome above her head. Skye ducked, shielding Carly's head with her hand. "Which way do we go?"

"Down here."

They jumped off the metal platform onto the concrete floor below. The vats towered over their heads like giant, steaming cauldrons. Hiding behind one, James pressed a panel, and a hatch opened to reveal a chute lined with a greasy substance.

"No. I'm not going down there." Even Skye had her limits.

"They won't follow us," James replied. "Guaranteed."

"How can you be so sure?"

"There's no easy way back, and they wouldn't want to miss their ship."

Skye considered a ride down the chute as the laser fire multiplied. The metal grating clanked above them as the men neared. Every moment the dark chute looked better.

James gave her a half smile full of mischief. "Surely, a

woman who hangs off a balcony three floors up isn't afraid of a little slime?"

She gave him a sharp stare. "Oh, all right."

James gestured toward the chute like a chauffeur escorting someone to a diamond-studded hovercraft. "After you."

Skye lifted Carly and climbed in behind her. Before she could adjust to the darkness, James gave her a gentle shove, and she slid down with Carly between her legs.

"Wait, I'm not ready!"

The slick sides of the chute gave her no leverage, and her hands slipped as she tried to slow down. Carly shrieked, and Skye joined in. They flew off the chute into absolute darkness and splashed into chilly water. The world muted. Carly's screams were gargled by water, and Skye struggled to find which way was up.

The darkness was absolute. Panicking, Skye thrashed her arms until she broke the surface. She gulped in air and shouted Carly's name.

Water splashed to her right, sprinkling on her cheek. "I'm over here."

Skye swam toward Carly and felt the little girl's face in her hands. Relief rushed up in a wave. "Thank goodness you're all right. Where did you learn how to swim?"

"Watching *Beach Party Rules*."

Skye laughed, wrapping her arms around Carly. "Who knew *Beach Party Rules* would save your life? All those hours I thought you were wasting your brain."

"Does that mean you'll let me watch it all the time?"

"Absolutely not." She didn't want Carly growing up thinking life was cocktails and swimsuit parties, and that you had to look like a stick with giant breasts to get any attention. Besides, you had to know influential, famous people to get anywhere near a beach these days. "How about more *Sesame*

Quadrant? I thought you liked Kyro the alien bird."

"Yeah, but he doesn't go anywhere. *Beach Party Rules* is by the ocean. It's cyberlicious." She said the word *ocean* as though it were a mythical place. Skye wished she could take her there.

Even though Skye had to remind her to act like a big girl, in some ways she was growing up faster than Skye would have liked. "Where did you hear that word, cyberlicious?"

Carly shrugged and looked down. "From *Beach Party Rules*."

"Of course." They found a spot where the water was shallow enough to stand up and waited for James. Their clothes dripped in the darkness, creating a rhythmic *plink plop*.

"What if he doesn't come?" Carly whispered. She had about as much faith in strangers as Skye had in Grease's promises…but James wasn't a stranger any longer, was he?

"Then we're stuck in some pitch-black underground sewer. At least there aren't any moonshiners down here." Skye's heart sped up. Maybe there were.

"James!" she yelled at the chute as if the rage in her voice alone would bring him down.

Silence, and then more *plink plop*. Doubt crept in, like the chill of the water catching hold to her bones. What if he didn't make it? Skye swallowed and summoned her courage. "Come on, Carls, Spread your arms. Search for a way out."

The chute clanged as if the door had opened and closed. At first Skye thought the guards had locked them in. Or would James do that to keep them safe? A rattling came next. Someone whooshed down.

Was it one of the guards? She grabbed Carly and backed into the corner. "Stay still and don't say anything until I do."

Carly grabbed her hand and nodded against her chest.

Her little fingers were frozen, and Skye rubbed her hands over them. Not that hers were any warmer.

The person in the chute came down with a splash beside them. Skye held her breath. Long moments passed before he surfaced and gasped for air.

"Skye? Carly?"

She released her breath in relief. "James, we're over here."

The water rippled as he swam closer. "Are you all right?"

"Wet and cold, but otherwise alive."

"Good." He found their incline and waded toward them. She wanted to reach out and feel him just to know he was there and not some imaginary hope. She held out her hand, feeling the air before her. But he didn't move, surprising her. He'd just held her hand through the entire party upstairs. Why not now?

"What's the plan? Carly and I were just feeling around for a way out."

"There's something I have to show you, Skye." His voice was serious and steady, as if he'd planned it all along. Her heart jumped. Would he tell her now he was a monster in disguise? No, not James the hero.

"What?" she shrieked.

She sensed movement in the darkness, like he had pulled something from his pocket. The room erupted in neon green light. As her eyes adjusted, she could discern a low ceiling, two channels running out into corridors beside them, and James, his head glowing like a light bulb, illuminating everything within ten feet.

"Cyber beans!" Carly whispered below her.

Skye yanked her hand back against her chest. Betrayal burned in her heart, despite the fact that he'd never promised her anything. She'd thought he was a hero, but he was no better than Grease, another gang member struggling through lower-level life. Actually, he was worse, the sworn enemy of the Razornecks. "You're with the Radioactive Hand of Justice?"

"I'm sorry I didn't have time to tell you. I know Carly's dad, your husband—"

"Boyfriend."

"Boyfriend," he amended. "You told me he's a Razorneck."

Her tone turned cool. "That would make us enemies."

"I don't want to be your enemy. I want to help you."

Skye's head whirled like someone had turned her upside down. She clung to what she knew. "That's what the Radioactive gangmen do—they help everyone out. But some people don't want your meager offerings. They want to pave their own way in the world."

"I understand that. What we have issue with is how they do it. They can't just take things for themselves and not share it with others."

"You'd turn into another government. Before you knew it, the handouts would run dry. Just like they did years ago."

"We don't want that. We want the people to rule."

"That's not what I've heard."

The air fizzled with dissonance between them. Grease used to love to talk about how the Radioactive Hand of Justice would be another useless government. Telling people what to do and how to do it. Rewarding some with food while punishing others they didn't think deserved it. How could she trust James?

What choice did she have?

Carly broke the silence as if his affiliations didn't matter. "Can we go now?"

James offered his hand, his palm shining in the light of his gang's colors. "I want to help you, Skye. My people found an unfinished colony ship. We can get you out of here if you're willing to come with us. If not, I can show you the way. You can go back to your apartment and wait for your boyfriend. But you have to evacuate this city one way or another. Once the moonshiners take over—and they will—the world leaders will deem this area contaminated and nuke it. Nothing in this city will live."

Skye shivered as she listened to his words. She'd grown to hate the Razornecks, but to go against them completely and side with the enemy was a risky move. Was the Radioactive Hand of Justice any better?

Underneath all her misgivings, she knew she still trusted James. How could a man that went out of his way to save them, and allowed them to tag along to the point where they'd jeopardize his mission be bad news?

She hated to admit it to herself, but she liked him. Going with him was the best for Carly, hands down. He made more of an effort to keep her safe than Grease had done in the three years she'd known him. Besides, he'd saved her and Carly, and she owed it to him to help him out.

"So are you with me or not?" James's hand didn't move.

Skye's heart was a storm of vulnerability. James radiated more than just neon light, and she felt like a moth drawn to his flame. She'd never felt this way about Grease. And yet, he'd ripped her heart out when he left. To have feelings for someone else so soon after Grease left scared her more than the thought of moonshiners at her door.

If she weren't careful, she'd hurt herself in more ways than one. But James was all they had, and she needed to put Carly first. Steeling herself, she stepped forward and slipped her hand in his. "I am."

"Good." He looked away as if collecting his emotions, and then pointed with his free hand. "This way."

Chapter Seven

A Piece of Paradise

James's hair reflected off the rippling water, casting ghostly light down the corridor. In the darkest, deepest passageways of Earth, he thought of Mestasis flying a parsec away, barreling through star-studded deep space.

Did she think of him? Or did steering the ship consume all her energy? In a way he wished it did, because she wouldn't have to bear the ache plaguing his own heart. But he also yearned for her to remember him. Would she look back five hundred years from now, when his bones were dust, and the *Expedition* neared Paradise 18? She'd be more machine than woman, absorbed into the mainframe to sustain her so she could continue to drive the ship. Would she think of him then?

Skye and Carly splashed behind him, stealing his thoughts from the heavens to the sewer. Skye's decision to go with him brought him immense relief. He couldn't imagine a young woman and a little girl wandering through the breached city to that trashed apartment, waiting for a Razorneck who probably wouldn't come home. The Radioactive Hand of

Justice would take them in despite their affiliation. With him they'd have a better life.

If I can get to the ship in time.

James squelched his doubt. When there was no room for error, he didn't make mistakes. Everything was going according to plan. He still had the miniscreen with the flying program and the coordinates, and he'd made it to the center of the city where Thadious Legacy's tower stood. Next he had to find a hovercraft.

Saving Skye and Carly brought him a measure of happiness against all the turmoil raging inside his chest. He liked Skye. Almost too much. Enough for guilt to coat every word he said to her. Mestasis was his love, and no one else could ever come close. Yet, Skye deserved better than a dingy apartment and boyfriend who would never come back. She was lovely and tough, with a princess-like grace and a strong sense of self. She could hang from a balcony and trudge through the sewers all to save a little girl who wasn't hers to begin with. The way she cared for Carly showed him how tender and loving her heart could be. She and Carly deserved their own paradise, and he wanted to give it to them.

More reason to get moving.

James quickened his pace as the air grew warmer, signaling they were walking below the next building: Thadious Legacy's tower. He spotted metal rungs on the cement and put up his hand for Skye and Carly to stop sloshing around.

"What is it?" Skye whispered, joining his side.

"I'm listening."

"For what?"

"Movement."

She put her hands on her hips, green eyes gleaming. "I thought you said there wouldn't be any guards."

"That's not who I'm listening for."

The moonshiners may have beaten them to it. If so, he wasn't about to emerge in a room full of speeding maniacs. But the upper levels were silent. With Morpheus charging the moonshiners' systems, there was no way they could keep still for that long.

"I think the coast is clear."

James climbed first, lifting a metal grating just enough to peer out of the hole. The basement could have been a royal throne room. High ceilings jutted in shadows with hanging crystal chandeliers. The floor was black-and-white checkered marble, contrasting with floral tapestries on the walls. An antique Lamborghini Reveneton rested on a pedestal under a clear plastic cover.

"We're definitely in the right place." James pushed the grating aside and hefted himself up. He offered Carly his hand, wondering if she'd finally accept his help.

Carly shot him a wary look. She may have realized she didn't have a choice, because her little hand darted up and she grabbed on. He lifted her, careful not to squeeze her hand too hard, yet she let go immediately after finding her footing and scurried a few feet away. James sighed. At least he'd made some sort of headway. Maybe next time she'd actually talk to him.

James offered his hand to Skye as Carly looked around.

"Why does the hovercraft have wheels on it?" Carly lifted the corner of the cover and touched the orange painted body.

"It's not a hovercraft, Carls, it's a car," Skye said, regaining her balance as James pulled her up.

"What's a car?"

Skye looked at James as if it was a tough question to answer. James tried to explain. "A long time ago, there weren't as many buildings, and people had room to drive on the land instead of riding in the air."

"Where did everyone live?"

Her question impressed him. She was a smart little girl for someone not educated in the high-rise Academies. "There weren't as many people back then, so we didn't have as many buildings."

"Oh."

Skye took Carly's hand. "Come on. We need to help James find a hovercraft."

"It's okay." James waved his hand. "I'm still thinking about the quickest way up. Legacy would have parked the hovercrafts on the higher levels, maybe even on the roof."

Before he could search for an elevator, Carly screamed, the sound shrill and full of terror. James whipped around and drew out his laser, pointing the barrel at a set of yellow, glassy eyes. The beast stood a whole foot taller than Carly, with white whiskers as long as her arm and a black and orange striped hide.

"It's stuffed," Skye said, putting her hand gently on James's arm. "The thing's probably been dead for over a century."

James sighed in relief and lowered his laser. "I think I've seen too many of those moonshiners. They've got me jumpy."

"We're all jumpy," Skye said with a sympathetic smile. She squeezed his arm before removing her hand. Before he could respond, she jogged over to Carly. "It's called a tiger—an animal that used to live on Earth. Go ahead, touch its fur."

Carly reached out, cringing at the same time. "It's soft."

"See? Nothing to be afraid of."

While they petted the stuffed tiger, James searched for a way up. "I think I see an elevator across the room."

His hopes rose, and he had to remind himself Thadious Legacy may have shut off the power.

"Great! Let's get out of here." Skye sounded triumphant.

James kept his own voice flat. "This tower's three hundred levels. Let's hope it still works."

They scuffled over the marble floor, leaving a trail of sludge from the sewers. James pressed the panel, and the numbers lit up. His mood brightened. Thadious Legacy had never struck him as an environmentalist. Made sense he wouldn't think to save energy for the rest of the world.

They stepped in and he pushed the level for the atrium that Mestasis had spoken of. His stomach grumbled, and he couldn't imagine how Skye and Carly felt. He had promised the little girl food, and he always kept his promises.

Elegant music played on the intercom system as the elevator rose. Sweet strings swelled in a melancholy melody accompanied by flute trills. The serene ambiance contrasted with the dire situation, making James feel as though Thadious Legacy mocked him from space.

Skye locked eyes with his, steadying him, helping him to refocus his thoughts. "I hope there's a hovercraft here."

"He has everything else: classical music, antique cars, chandeliers—you'd think he'd have at least one utility vehicle."

"If you look hard enough, you just may find another colony ship somewhere on one of these levels. Heck, maybe even another planet."

"Yeah, stashed right next to the crystal wine glasses."

Skye shrugged. "We might as well just stay here, invite your friends, have a party."

James chuckled. "I've never heard you use sarcasm."

"Just wait. You have a lot to learn about me." Her eyes teased him.

"Good stuff, I hope."

"Depends on what you'd call good."

Carly pulled on Skye's shirt, interrupting. "I don't want to stay here. The music is scary."

Skye smoothed her hand over the stray wisps of blond in Carly's hair. "Don't worry, Carls. We're not staying long."

The elevator beeped, and a smooth voice announced, "Level Two-hundred and forty-three. Enjoy."

A wave of humid air hit them in the face like a tropical bath, smelling of sweet blossoms. Vines draped in front of them, and James pulled the greenery back for them to enter. The walls were made of glass. Sparkling stars winked at them in the velvety black sky. Even this floor rose above the city lights.

"What is this place?" Skye's eyes widened.

James averted his eyes from the stars and who they reminded him of. He pulled an apple hanging from the branch of a tree, feeling the smooth peel under his fingers. "Pit stop for lunch."

"Smokin' cyber beans!" Carly took off, jogging down a row of fruit trees. She stopped and grabbed a cherry, probing it with her fingers until the skin broke and juice flowed out. "Is it really real?"

"Carls, don't eat that. It might be poisonous."

"She's fine," James assured her, taking a bite of the apple. The sweet tartness stung his tongue. "This is Thadious Legacy's private greenhouse, used to grow all his own food."

She watched him swallow the bite. He saw her calculating behind her sharp eyes, weighing the risk against her own hunger.

"I guess if it was good enough for him, then it's good enough for me." She knelt down and pulled a tomato off a spindly vine.

He threw her an apple, shining in the moonlight, bright as a new toy. "Eat as much as you can and fill your pockets. I'm not sure when we'll have more food."

"Like this? Probably never," Skye said as she bit into the

tomato and juices flowed down her chin. She brought her hand up to stop it and looked back at him sheepishly, as if there were table manners in an abandoned greenhouse at the end of the world.

James smiled. His gaze flitted to where the juice ran down her chin to her neck and he turned away, embarrassed. How could he notice such things when Mestasis was off flying the ship with input holes drilled into her head? He busied himself by picking fruit for the ride.

"Look what I found, Skye!" Carly dangled a carrot by the roots. Moist soil clung to her little fingers. Cherry juice stained her lips, and she'd stuffed her cheeks to bursting with berries.

After filling his pockets with apples and oranges, James found Skye digging up potatoes with her fingers. "I'm going hovercraft hunting. You and Carly stay here and rest. I'll come get you if I find anything."

"Sure thing." Skye flashed a reassuring smile and held his eyes with her own. "Be careful."

Her words hung heavily in the air between them. He wondered if her concern ran deeper than the fact she needed him to save her and Carly's life. The urge to comfort her grew inside him. He had always been a caretaker, and Skye's vulnerable position drew him in. James ran his finger along her cheek, wiping away a streak of tomato juice. As he touched her, an insistent pain ached inside him.

Not again.

Romance couldn't snare him twice. Losing Mestasis had almost killed him, and he never wanted to reopen that wound. Caretaking was one thing, loving, another.

He pulled back, his voice cold. "I'll return soon."

Just as he turned to step away, the elevator beeped, a jarring sound invading their private pocket of paradise. He jerked his head up, watching as the doors closed and the platform plunged to the lower levels.

"Is it returning to Level One automatically?" Skye's voice cracked. Her fingers trembled, dropping the potato. It bounced once and landed by James's boot.

"Not sure." James slipped out his laser. "One way to find out."

They waited as the numbers on the panel decreased. It took ten minutes for the platform to reach the bottom, but neither of them moved. Carly hummed in the background, skipping among the berry bushes. The beeps ceased as the platform reached ground level..

James held his breath, feeling like he'd sucked a storm inside his chest. A burst of new electricity buzzed, and the elevator rose with a new series of beeps.

Skye gasped and whispered as if the intruder could hear her from three hundred levels below, "Someone's coming."

James raised the laser to the door. "Let them come."

Chapter Eight

Promise

Skye felt like a credit thief caught with their fake card inserted in the Automatic Transfer Module. She knew Thadious Legacy had flown away, never to come back again. So who was in on their little plan?

"Carly," she whispered to get her attention. "Hide in the bushes. Someone's coming."

Each beep increased her adrenaline by exponential increments, shaking her limbs down to the tips of her fingers. She picked up the potato from the ground and held it in her fist, ready to aim.

Level Two-hundred and forty-one.

Two-hundred and forty-two.

Her fingernails dug into her palm. Maybe they'd keep going, right on up to the roof. The final beep rocked her very core as the doors parted.

A man hobbled out like an anticlimactic end to a scene in *Beach Party Rules*. His shoulders slumped forward and grimy brown hair fell in front of his eyes. One hand jerked in a twitching motion, while the other waved as if he painted circles in the air.

"Daddy!" Before Skye could react, Carly dashed out from the bushes and scurried toward the elevator.

Skye stood up in utter shock, hope and disbelief tingling through her like she'd awoken from a beautiful dream. The potato slipped from her fingers.

"Grease?"

He didn't answer her. Carly stopped two feet in front of him and paused, as if she sensed there was something wrong. Her voice still held hope. "I knew you'd come back."

"I promised ya, didn't I?" His voice was scratchy, as if he hadn't used it in a long time. "Too bad Skye didn't believe me."

He held up her note in his shuddery hand. "I followed you all the way here, tracking your footsteps through the sewers." His head jerked, and she saw a line of black snaking down his chin. "I can smell a lot of things now: the sweat of fear, the reek of a drop of blood, the tracks of a betrayer."

Skye threw her arms up, palms outstretched. "Grease, I can explain. I watched the footage of the attack so many times. I thought you were dead."

His shoulders squiggled as if scorpions were running up his back. "So you ran off with another man, a do-gooder leprechaun, the enemy of the Razornecks." Bitterness dripped from his words.

Skye crashed inside. It hurt to have him see her like this. He believed she'd abandoned what they'd had. "I waited for you for hours until we had no food left and a crazy old woman ransacked our apartment."

"Looks like you hightailed it outta there first chance you got, first man you met."

Grease's twitching increased in speed until he shuffled

from foot to foot. Everything about him was wrong; the way he stood with his back bent forward, the hatred in his voice, the strange movement of his hands. All those hours she'd wished for him to come back, and now his presence twisted her stomach. She pitied him, missed him, and feared him all at the same time.

Maybe some promises are better left unfinished.

Grease reached out and grabbed Carly in the twitch of a finger. He held her close, like a rag doll he'd reclaimed from a stolen loot pile.

Carly shrieked, tears running down her cheeks. Jennifer fell to the floor, the doll's eyes lolling.

Grease's hands tightened around her. "I'm not going to let you take my family away from me."

James held up his hand, gripping the laser in the other. "Let her go, Grease, and we'll work this all out."

"There's nothing..." Grease paused as if he'd lost his train of thought and shook his head. "To work out."

Grease moved from side to side like a predator deciding how and when to strike. He raised his head and his hair fell back, revealing a charred streak of flesh running down his cheek to his neck. His weasel-like black eyes shifted. As Skye looked into them, the darkness spread to the corners. They looked too big and slanted in a strange, alien way.

"You've got to do something," Skye whispered through trembling lips. "He's different than he used to be. He's *changed*."

James shook his head. "I can't hurt Carly's father. No matter what he's become."

Grease retreated toward the elevator. "I'm taking Carly with me. You can stay with your new boyfriend. I don't need ya."

James tightened his grip on the trigger. "I can't let you do that."

He fired and Skye screamed. The white light flashed by Grease and Carly, hitting the elevator panel. The wires short-circuited, and the doors sealed shut.

James held the laser steady. "Now let's have a friendly talk—"

But before he could finish, Grease tossed Carly aside. She sprawled through the air and hit the glass wall with a *thunk*, sliding down to the ground with her face in the soil. Grease bolted at James. His head crashed into James's stomach, and the laser careened across the greenhouse, landing in a bush.

Skye sprinted to Carly, feeling every nightmare she'd ever had springing to life. She turned Carly's head over and felt her neck for a pulse. A raised welt appeared on her forehead, but her heartbeat was steady. Holding the little girl in her arms, Skye watched James and Grease tumble into the pumpkin patch.

James was an excellent fighter. She'd witnessed his skills firsthand when he punched the guard in the face, but the moonshine in Grease's veins gave him extraordinary speed. He punched James in the cheek before James could bring up his arm to defend himself, and then buried his head in James's shoulder. James screamed in pain.

Skye placed Carly down and dived in the bushes for the laser. If she didn't stop Grease, he'd kill James and come after her and Carly next. Thorns cut her arms as she dug through the brambles.

It's got to be here somewhere. She'd seen it fly into the bush as she ran after Carly.

The moonlight trickled down through the weaving branches, illuminating a black sheen that had to be the barrel. Skye thrust her hand into the soil and yanked the laser out of the bush. She'd never held a real one before, and it felt heavy and cold in her hands. The photon stimulator vibrated underneath her fingertips. The gun was charged and ready to go.

When she turned around, Grease was hovering over James, digging through the pockets of his torn coat with blood dripping from his chin. He pulled out a switchblade and flipped it open, the silver blade catching the moon's rays.

"No!" Skye shouted, pointing the laser in his direction. "Grease, stop."

Grease turned to face her, the skin on his face dark as night. She wondered if the fire had caused the discoloring, or if the moonshine had traveled all the way up his arm. His eyes were cold and empty as if he struggled to remember his own name. He turned on James and raised the blade.

Skye pulled the trigger and the barrel exploded into light. The shaft hit Grease in the chest, and he fell back from the force. She ran to James, still holding the laser. Blood covered his arm from his shoulder to his chest. He shouted, his voice filled with pain. "Keep firing!"

No normal human could have survived that laser wound. Grease rose, the flames produced by the laser licking up the clothes on his chest. His skin burned black where she'd hit him, making Skye's heart cringe. Could she really fire at him again? He scrambled toward her, barring his teeth. If she didn't fire, he'd topple her over and bite her next. Carly needed her, and she had to get back to the little girl. Steeling her nerves, Skye fired multiple rounds, each shot like a dagger in her gut, softening her resolve but barely slowing him down.

Think of Carly. You have to protect her.

Fingers shaking, she raised the laser and aimed for his head. A thousand memories flew through her mind: Grease's quirky smile when he first saw her in the alleyway, his protective hand on Carly's shoulder, the way he slouched on the couch while watching the holoscreen. This shot would end it all. Part of her doubted she could pull the trigger, but the orphan-survivor inside her had no hesitations.

Skye fired, and it was like shooting at her own head. The streak of light seized Grease like a lightning bolt and he fell to the soil, unmoving. Time stopped, her breath ripped out of her chest. The finality of the moment smacked her in the face. Her hands trembled as she brought down the laser and it fell to the ground. Her body turned to grains of sand, and she collapsed on her knees, crawling toward Carly.

The little girl lay sideways in the soil with one eye covered in sand. Skye turned her on her back, brushed off her face, and felt her breath. Small puffs of air blew on Skye's hand, and relief turned her whole body into mush. She fell on her back beside Carly and started to cry, watching the stars glitter like diamonds of hope in the sky.

James. He'd saved them both from Grease and may have lost him own life in return. Skye jolted up and stumbled toward him. James sat, holding a piece of his shirt over his shoulder to stop the bleeding.

Worry filled his eyes. "Is Carly okay?"

Skye nodded. "She's breathing, but she's knocked out cold."

"Thank goodness, she's okay." His shoulders slumped in relief. "It might be better this way. I don't want her seeing her dad like this."

Skye knelt beside him and put pressure on the wound. The feel of hot blood under her fingers made her stomach twist with worry. *How bad is it?* Did she have the courage to even ask?

James gave her an incredulous look. "Skye, you saved my life."

"Grease would have killed us all."

"I know. I'm just so impressed." He touched her cheek with his good arm. "You were really brave."

Skye waved his comment off. She felt like a murderer. "Grease bit you, didn't he?" she said in resignation as she wound the piece of shirt around her arm and tied a knot.

"Several times."

She could barely speak. "Will you be all right?"

He winced, unable to hide the truth from his face. "I'm not sure."

Skye covered her face with her hands. Her world was tumbling down on top of her, and she had no way to hold it up. She'd just lost Grease all over again, James was wounded—possibly infected—and Carly had been knocked unconscious.

James put a hand on her arm. "The Morpheus in his blood could have infected me, but I'm not sure it's enough to have any lasting effect. I'm alive, thanks to you, and that's what matters now."

He sat up and gently pulled her hands off her eyes. "You did the right thing, Skye. Never think any differently."

Her stomach sickened with the fresh memory of Grease dying from her own hand. She hadn't been able to keep him from leaving, but she didn't think twice about stopping him now. Was she more fit to kill than to love?

James brought her out of her brooding thoughts. "We have to get Carly and find a hovercraft before the city falls."

She helped him up, and they jogged to the soil where Carly lay. The girl looked like a fallen angel, an innocent being brought into a hellish world.

James lifted Carly in his arms. "Come on, we've made enough noise to attract all the moonshiners in the city. Let's get out of here."

Skye nodded, refusing to think he hurried because *he* may not have much time left.

Chapter Nine

Courage of Love

Holding Carly in his arms, guilt spread through James like an infection. He shouldn't have allowed the situation to get out of hand. Compassion was his greatest weakness, and he'd paused when Carly called out to her father. He should have relied on his instincts and shot the man dead on the spot. But that's what separated the Radioactive Hand of Justice from the Razornecks—placing others above your own needs. Besides, Skye seemed to hold out hope from the initial expression on her face.

His shoulder ached and the skin was rubbed raw underneath his shirt where Grease's teeth had punctured the flesh. Instead of feeling dizzy from loss of blood, energy flowed through him, making him hyperaware of every smell and every motion. He hoped the rush was adrenaline, but a little voice in his head whispered his newfound sensitivity resulted from something more.

"How are you feeling?" Skye asked between huffs as they climbed another flight of stairs to the roof.

"Doing fine." He didn't want to upset her, and he had no evidence to say otherwise. People exposed themselves to Morpheus for months before showing any moonshiner symptoms, yet blood-to-blood transfusion may be different altogether. His anxiety rose when he considered it, so he pushed his worries far from his mind. He had to focus on the mission and get them out of the city to Project Exodus.

They reached another platform, and Skye pushed open the emergency exit door enough to peer in.

"Looks like offices. Just a lot of desks and leather chairs."

James shifted Carly in his arms and stifled his disappointment. "Let's keep climbing. Doesn't sound worth the time to look."

The higher they climbed, the more he wondered how self-sufficient Thadious Legacy's Tower was. Maybe he didn't need hovercrafts at all. If so, James had trapped them in the middle of a fallen city at the end of the world. Chances were he could get them back to the bunker, but what then? Wait in a cement box for the rest of his life?

James pushed ahead, taking advantage of his new well of energy. With him carrying Carly, Skye could keep up with his pace. They checked every floor, and it took them an hour to reach the roof.

They stood in front of the emergency exit like souls waiting at the gates of heaven, unsure of their own salvation.

"This is it." James glanced at Skye for her permission to reveal what lay beyond the door.

Skye's harried nudge of her chin told him she was tired of anticipation. He wondered how long she'd been waiting in her life to do something about her situation before finally hanging off that balcony. Well, she was acting now.

"Push it open. I'm ready."

James leaned his weight against the door, and they

stepped out, the night sky twinkling above them. Their feet sunk into white sand trailing down to water.

"What? A lake? On top of a building?"

"It's a swimming pool," James said in disgust, wondering why someone would waste sun space that could be used for growing food.

"You mean for fun?" Skye circled the pool, looking down into the placid water.

"Guess so."

"Wait a second. I know this place." Skye's eyes widened. "This is where they shot *Beach Party Rules*." *It wasn't an actual beach. It was all a lie.*

James shrugged, not caring about Thadious Legacy's pastime hobbies. In a few hours, the World Coalition was going to reduce the whole city to dust. His eyes scanned the length of the building and rested on two duel twin engines the size of subway tunnels. Above them, a sight panel stretched out in the shape of a visor. The metal glinted in the moonlight like a polished prize.

It was the largest, and most thoroughly decked out hovercraft he'd ever seen.

"That what you're looking for?" Skye glanced back at him with a pleased smirk on her face.

"I'll settle for that, yes." James handed Carly to Skye and hurried around the pool to see if he could make sense of the controls. He pulled his miniscreen from his backpack, and plugged it into the panel in the driver's side. With a few pats of his finger, the hatch opened, revealing a cockpit full of buttons and blinking lights. An alarm beeped, and James waved to Skye to get on board. The guards were long gone, but such a noise would draw moonshiners like moths to a light stick.

"Can you fly it?" Skye climbed up beside him, holding

Carly close.

"Yeah, of course." Such a vehicle was the product of his dreams. In his mind, he'd been flying it all his life. The hatch closed, and he settled into the pilot's seat. Using his miniscreen, he downloaded the system controls and input the coordinates Dal had given him. While waiting for his processor to analyze the data, he sent a message to Dal.

HOVERCRAFT ACQUIRED. EN ROUTE TO PROJECT EXODUS.

He could picture the old man smiling three hundreds levels down.

The miniscreen beeped and a map appeared along with a bright yellow line leading to the coordinates in the Barrens. James pulled back a lever, and the engines rumbled below them like awakened giants, sending fake beach sand into the air. The ship tilted slightly as it rose up and hovered over the pool, creating ripples in the water below them.

James took the controls, and they sped off the roof of the building, shooting up into the night sky. The streets below scurried with motion. James shone a honing light down between the buildings. Moonshiners piled on top of one another, reaching to the sky. He shrugged off a shiver and pulled up, glad to leave the city.

The high-rises grew small underneath them, some buildings lit up like fireflies, and others black as death. He passed over the charred remains of the State Building, thinking of Grease and pitying him.

Skye came in and slipped into the seat next to him, securing her belt. "Carly woke up, but went right back to sleep, so I belted her in lying down."

He turned toward her, taking his eyes off the sky to give her an encouraging smile. "Don't worry, Skye; she'll be okay."

Skye's shoulders rose and fell as if the weight of all the levels she'd lived under pressed on top of her. "It's my fault."

To have Skye feel even a little bit at fault for anything that had happened made James angry with himself. She was a victim of poor circumstances, nothing more. He was a trained gang member who took an oath to defend the helpless.

"Nothing is your fault. I should have acted faster. I could have shot him before he got to Carly."

"No. You did the right thing." Skye held his eyes in a firm lock with her own. "I, on the other hand, started this whole mess and dragged Carly into it."

"You did what you had to do to keep her safe. Grease made his own choices, none of them wise."

"I never loved him, not like I should have." She blurted it out and James looked away, not knowing how to respond.

From the corner of his eye, he could see her gazing into the distance, where the city ended and the Barrens began. "He found me scavenging in an alley. I'd grown too old for the orphanage, so I took to the streets, scrounging to stay alive. I was starving, and he offered me shelter and a hot meal. I thought I'd stay for a night, nothing more. Then, I met Carly and learned her mother had left before she could remember. I was the only woman she'd ever met. I'd always wanted to be a mother. I couldn't leave her."

Skye shifted uncomfortably. "I grew to care for Grease as well, but I never truly loved him the way I loved Carly. I feel so awful saying it."

"You can't choose who you love," James said, thinking of his instant connection to Mestasis, his tragic love story. "Your heart chooses for you."

"Well, my heart must have been on vacation, because if

I loved him enough, I would have found the courage to stop him. I wouldn't have let him go."

"You can't keep people locked up. You can't prevent them from fulfilling their own destinies, their own dreams." He loved Mestasis so much he'd wanted her to go, and she couldn't have kept him from his own inclinations to save more people in the crumbling world.

James continued. "People have to make their own choices in life. It doesn't mean you don't love him, or he you."

She jerked up, looking at James as if she saw him for the first time. Her eyebrows rose. "The *Expedition*."

He could see her thinking, see in her glittering eyes as she connected fragments of who she knew he was. "A woman you loved took off on that colony ship, didn't she?"

James focused on the sky ahead, wondering how his heart could be so transparent. Confirming the truth would only reopen the sore, yet he couldn't deny her. She'd saved his life and helped him find the hovercraft. She had a right to know. "Yes."

"What is her name?"

"Mestasis."

It felt so good to say it out loud, as if he could conjure her next to him with only the sound of those syllables he'd uttered in moments of ecstasy and pain.

"A beautiful name." Skye sat back against her seat.

James fell silent, hoping she'd drop the conversation, but apparently she was only gathering her courage to ask the next question.

"Why didn't you go with her?"

He took a deep breath and let it out slowly. How could he put his experience into words she'd understand? "They did extensive DNA testing to ensure healthy future generations on the ship. I didn't make the cut."

"You seem very capable to me."

His lips curved up at the compliment, but his smile didn't last. "I have a heart arrhythmia, and they didn't think I'd survive the pressures of living in a low-gravity environment. Besides, my genes had latent diseases that were sure to manifest in future generations."

"Bad genes, my ass." Skye sniffed haughtily. "If I loved the person, I wouldn't care what DNA he had."

"Unfortunately, that's not how Thadious Legacy views the world."

Skye's eyes were fierce, like she could never forgive this woman she hadn't even met. "Why didn't she stay?"

"She'd signed a contract with Thadious Legacy himself. She and her sister were to pilot the ship in exchange for tickets for three hundred of my people."

"Wow. And if she didn't go?"

"He'd call off the bargain. Three hundred people would go back to the sewers. Her sister would have to drive the ship without her."

"How awful."

"You're telling me." James shifted in his seat. As much as the topic pained him, it helped to get it out in the open, as if sharing his hurt with Skye would share the burden as well.

"James, I'm so sorry."

He appreciated her sympathy, but it wasn't necessary—she had enough to worry about. He waved it off. "It couldn't have happened any other way. I realized if I *had* taken off on that ship, I couldn't have ever forgiven myself. Yes, I'd be overseeing three hundred of my own people, but what about all the others I'd leave behind? No, I was meant to be here, Skye, to pilot that colony ship and save the people left in the city. I accept my destiny. I embrace it."

She spoke softly, as if she was afraid of the question and

his answer. “Yes, but will you ever be able to let Mestasis go?”

James shrugged, looking down at his hands on the controls. Why did it matter so much to her?

“Only time will tell.”

Chapter Ten

False Hero

"Where are we?" Carly's voice wafted up from the back of the hovercraft in a soft murmur, barely audible against the roar of the engines.

Skye whipped around in her seat. "She's awake."

She fumbled with the buckles as James pressed something on the panels controlling the ship and leaned over to help her with her restraints. His hands brushed against hers as he popped the buckle open on the first try. They hustled to the backseat where Carly lay. For Skye, seeing her eyes open was like seeing light after a century of darkness.

"Carly, are you feeling okay?"

"My head hurts." She put her hand up to her forehead and felt the bump. "What happened? Where are we?"

"We're on a hovercraft. We made it out of the city, Carls." Skye tried to keep things positive, wondering if she'd remember anything that had happened. "We're headed toward a big ship in the Barrens."

"Where's Daddy?"

Her heart sank to her feet. The ugly truth sat on her tongue like poison. How could she tell her? "What do you remember?"

Carly rubbed her eyes. "I don't know."

The roar of the engines beneath them heightened the anticipation. Skye didn't want to say anything right now if she could help it. Her finger brushed the lump on the little girl's forehead. "You need to rest."

Carly's gaze wandered around the cabin area and focused on something far away. "I had the strangest dream. We were in a greenhouse, and I'd just eaten so many berries, my stomach hurt. Then I saw Daddy. He was sick."

Skye's fingers shook. "What else do you remember?"

"That's it. Where's Daddy?" This time her question came out as a demand.

Skye looked to James, pleading for some miracle.

James nodded as if he knew how to handle it. He leaned over. "Your daddy was very brave, but he didn't make it, honey."

"What?" Carly's chin trembled. She put both hands on her head and scrunched up her hair in her fists.

James placed a hand on Carly's shoulder. "He couldn't come with us."

"Why?" Her voice squeaked as her face fell apart.

Skye watched as James thought over his response.

His face turned from apologetic to resolute. "Your father loved you very much, and he wanted you to be safe. He tried hard for you but he didn't make it."

Carly wiggled out of James's touch and looked at him as if he were a demon. "You left him there?"

Skye interrupted. "No he didn't, Carls. James helped as well."

Shooting upright, Carly stuck a finger at James. "I wish

stupid green-hair had stayed behind instead."

"Carly, you don't mean that," Skye scolded her.

"Yes, I do." Tears flowed down her cheeks and she blinked to see through them. "I hate him, and I miss my daddy."

"Carls—"

She pulled away from Skye and ran into the cargo hold. Skye moved to go after her, but James put a gentle hand on her arm, holding her back. "Give her time."

Carly's pain stabbed Skye in the gut, and she held her stomach, wanting to shield Carly from the truth and shield James from Carly's wrath all at the same time—and failing at both endeavors. "Why didn't you tell her the whole truth?"

"I told her what she needed to hear. Her dad did love her, and he wanted to keep her safe. That's what she needs to know."

"But she'll hate you forever. She'll think you left him behind."

James smiled sadly. "What was I going to do? Tell her that her dad had turned into a monster? I'd rather her hate me and feel loved than have nightmares of what really happened. No child should see their parent like that."

"She's got to know the truth."

"We'll tell her someday when she's older. Right now, she's had enough heartache."

Skye looked deeply in his eyes, seeing emotion simmer inside the misty depths. "You care about her, too."

James opened his mouth to respond, but an alarm buzzed from the cockpit.

"I'm sorry." He darted back to his pilot seat as if fleeing laser fire.

Torn between helping Carly and finding out what was wrong, Skye followed him. Carly needed time to cool off, and Skye couldn't help her if she didn't know what they faced.

She slipped into the cockpit and leaned over James's shoulder. He tapped on one of the panels and flicked a few switches.

"What is it?"

"Drained energy cell. Looks like our good friend, TL, didn't mean to fly this ship very far."

Skye searched the horizon. Nothing but the husks of abandoned buildings cluttered the ground. Dust blew everywhere. The desert had taken the land. "What are we going to do?"

"Look for something to power the ship."

"And what if we can't find anything?"

James quirked an eyebrow. "We'll walk."

"In the middle of a desert?"

"If we have to. The nuclear fallout will contaminate this area as well. We need to keep moving."

"You really think they'll nuke it?"

"They blew up Utopia and the State building, didn't they?"

His words slapped her in the face, and she looked away, cheeks burning.

James reached out and squeezed her arm. "I'm sorry, I didn't mean to mention…"

She sniffed and put her hand to her mouth, waving him off. "It's not your fault, remember?"

James gripped the controls with white knuckles. "Someone's got to take responsibility for all that's wrong with the world."

Yes, but did it always have to be James? Skye wanted to share his burden, to help him achieve his goals, but could she really be a hero herself? It seemed like such an insurmountable task, and she had her own problems to work out.

She reached through all her weaknesses and pulled out a

kernel of courage. "I will." She spread her hands. "I just don't know how to start."

James looked up from the controls with intensity brewing like a storm in his eyes. "You've already given me more to fight for. I mean…you and Carly."

Heat blossomed from the back of her neck to her cheeks. The storm in James's eyes traveled to stir up emotions in her heart. *What does he mean?*

Skye wanted to press further, but her tongue wouldn't work. What he had with Mestasis sounded like true love, and who was she to intervene? Her eyes broke his turbulent gaze and sought refuge on the horizon.

A light appeared from the gray nothingness like a nugget of gold. Skye pointed, her finger pressing against the glass. "Look! Over there. I see something."

James turned the hovercraft toward it. "It's coming from a building."

"If they have light, then they'll have energy cells."

"Thing is, will they want to part with them?"

"Hell, yeah," Skye said with attitude. They had the ultimate bargaining chip. As an alley rat, Skye knew how to deal. "Offer them a ride off this planet, and they'll be begging at your feet."

He nodded, considering her advice. A spark in his eye told her she'd impressed him with her shrewdness. "Good idea." He flicked a switch and pulled a lever by his thigh. "I'm taking the ship down. It would be safer if you could get Carly to belt herself in."

Skye nodded, thinking it would be easier to command the heavens to save the planet. "I'll try."

Running to the back of the hovercraft, Skye found Carly sitting against a supply container, hugging her legs like a lost orphan, reminding Skye so much of herself at that age. Of course, Skye hadn't met either of her parents. At least Carly had a chance to get to know her dad. But Skye didn't know what was worse—never having parents, or having them taken away.

"We need to belt ourselves back in, Carls. We're landing."

Carly didn't move. "I don't care."

"Well, I do." Skye grabbed her arm and pulled her up. It was about time Skye started acting like a real mother. Sometimes that meant being the bad guy, just like James. "You're not turning into a hovercraft pancake."

The authority in Skye's voice worked. Carly dragged her feet to her seat and Skye belted them both in. The hovercraft sank underneath them, flipping her stomach. Carly's eyes widened as their hair fanned around their shoulders.

Skye reached out and squeezed her hand. "It's gonna be all right."

The buildings grew larger underneath them, turning a burned model village into a full-fledged war zone. Skye wanted to tell Carly about the beach where they'd filmed *Beach Party Rules*, but she figured it would just make Carly angrier she'd missed it. Instead, Skye settled for giving her a comforting smile.

After a smooth landing, the engines died down.

Skye squeezed Carly's hand. "See, we made it."

Carly started to smile, but then her face fell. Skye glanced up to see James looking more relieved than she thought he should after landing a dying hovercraft in the middle of nowhere.

James settled sideways into the seat in front of them. "I just got a message from my contact in the city. He said there're two more colony ships set to take off in the next few days, so we have more time than he initially thought. They won't nuke the city until the higher-ups have all made it out."

"What about the others who didn't make it on a ship?"

James shrugged. "Guess they'll have to come with us."

Skye smiled so much the muscles in her cheeks burned. Every minute she spent with James, she found another reason to like him. "The Radioactive Hand of Justice won't mind the company?"

"We welcome all."

"How did you get to be so heroic?" Although her tone was sarcastic, she was only half joking.

"Someone had to step up." James gave Carly a hesitant wink and stood up to pull some blankets from a cargo hold.

"We can rest until daylight. Moonshiners don't like sunlight, so it will be safer to travel through the buildings in the morning. Try to get a few hours of sleep."

Like Skye could sleep at all on a stolen hovercraft in the Barrens with a nuke ready to go off over their heads. She took a blanket and covered Carly as the little girl lay down across the back seat. The little girl still didn't speak to either of them, but Skye knew to give it time.

James checked the door lock and then slipped back into the pilot's seat. He spoke over his shoulder. "I'll keep watch."

"You don't need sleep?" Skye whispered. Carly had closed her eyes, and Skye wanted her to get as much rest as possible.

"Strangely, I'm not tired." He looked surprised, as if he didn't trust his own body. A rip current of anxiety rose inside her as her eyes flicked to his bandaged shoulder, but she said nothing.

What if I lose him, too?

She searched his eyes for any sign of blackness, but the misty silver color still mesmerized her.

His face softened as he caught her staring. "You should get some rest. You've had a busy day. I'll be all right at the helm."

The confidence in his voice only alleviated a sliver of her doubt. But she couldn't stand there and stare at him all night.

"Look." James stood up and walked toward her. He reached into his holster. "Here's my laser. If anything happens to me—"

"I can't." Skye avoided looking at the weapon.

"You saw what happened to Grease." James held it out, insistent. "You can give it back to me in the morning." His words sounded like a promise. So far, he'd always kept his end of a deal.

"Okay." Skye's hand rested on his for a long moment before she took the laser. She didn't feel comfortable handling a weapon again. "See you at dawn."

Swallowing her fear, Skye left him in the cockpit. She settled in next to Carly, like they'd done for the last three years, and closed her eyes. Her thoughts sped like hovercrafts in her head.

Grease is dead.

I killed him.

Reality stung her again and again, and she kept prying the truth open, as if through frequent exposure she'd come to terms with the ugly facts. Grief and pity mixed in her chest like a poisonous soup. The laser felt cold against her skin as she cradled it in her arms. Would she ever forgive herself?

I shot Grease to save Carly. There's nothing else I could have done.

Chapter Eleven

Diagnosis

Red splotches burned against the back of James's lids. He fought through grogginess and peeled open his eyes, staring down the sun as it crested the broken-toothed horizon of ruined buildings. How long had he been asleep?

He jumped to his feet, fighting dizziness to check on Carly and Skye. His miniscreen fell off his lap, the flight program designed to help him control the *Destiny* flashing a virtual crashed ship by his feet.

"Dammit!" He'd dozed off on his watch all the way until sunrise. That wasn't like him at all, and his momentary slip of control scared him more than the pain radiating underneath his arm.

Skye slept on her back, holding his laser in both her arms like a precious gift from a lover. Carly snuggled beside her. James paused, watching Skye's peaceful face. She never made such a serene expression while awake. Asleep, she looked like a Celtic princess under a spell. A tough Celtic princess; one who had saved his life.

He resisted the urge to leave her be. They needed to take advantage of the daylight. Stepping toward her, he slipped his fingers into her hand and squeezed. "Time to get up."

Skye shifted and blinked. Her face turned from angelic to suspicious and her hand darted to the laser.

James laughed and held up his hands. "I'm still here."

Her features crumpled into relief. She pulled herself up, her red hair falling around her shoulders. "How do you feel?"

"A little sleepy, but okay."

"Thank goodness." She looked like she was about to leap up and throw her arms around him, but she froze and handed him back his laser instead. An agenda formed in her green eyes. "Let's find the source of that light."

"Wake Carly. I'll scout the best way to get there."

She nodded and he reached into his pocket and handed her three oranges. "I know it's not a well-rounded breakfast..."

Skye smiled and scooped up the oranges. "We'll live. It's much better than old soycaroni."

He wrinkled his nose. "I *thought* your apartment smelled like burned pasta."

"Well, I'm not the best cook."

"But you're still the best mom I know."

Skye looked to the floor. "I'm waiting for the day Carly thinks so and calls me *Mom*." She laughed, looking more vulnerable than amused. "I guess I have to earn it first."

He felt the urge to put his arms around her, but his muscles tensed and he held back. He couldn't allow himself to get any closer to this woman. A deeper aching underlined his urge to comfort her, an aching he shouldn't have. Besides, with his hurt shoulder, who knew how long he had? And the fate of all those left behind was at stake. He couldn't allow himself to get distracted. While he was with Mestasis the whole city had fallen apart.

"I'll be right back."

James pressed the panel and the hatch opened with a whiff of stale, burned air. He jumped down and walked to the edge of the roof, his tenseness dissipating in the wind. The city smelled like ash and mold, and nothing but rats crawled in the alleys. Something had plowed through this part of the district, demolishing a chain of buildings and the corridors connecting to the one they'd landed on. He hadn't seen the wake of destruction in the darkness last night.

James followed the trail of debris to a crashed lunar freighter, the front hull crumpled against a building two blocks down.

"What happened here?" He jumped at Skye's voice as she poked her head out of the hatch, following his gaze to the ship. Had they already wolfed down those oranges?

"I guess it lost control." He tried to remember any news story about a lost lunar freighter, but for some reason, the government must have covered it up.

"Do you think it has a working energy cell?" She helped Carly jump from the hatch. The little girl clung to Skye's arm, her eyes shifty. James couldn't imagine what it would be like to learn your dad didn't make it, and you'd never see him again. He gave Carly an encouraging smile. She buried her head against Skye, and James went back to studying the ship.

"Probably not. Looks like it's been here for a while. I bet alley rats looted it right after the crash."

"So our best bet is to pay a visit to whomever still has that power source," Skye concluded, taking Carly's hand.

"You're right." James pointed three blocks down to a corridor the fallen ship hadn't smashed in. "And I think I found the quickest way."

"We're coming with you." Skye's gaze told him there'd be no way to dissuade her. "We're not staying in that hovercraft locked up, waiting for you to come back. As the only shiny thing within a hundred miles, it's a sitting duck, and you have the only working laser."

"You've got a point." James admired her determination. She had more bravado than some of the Radioactive trainees. "Come on. If we leave now, we'll reach it within the hour."

He gave the little girl a steady glance. "Carly, you ready?"

She nodded, pulling away from Skye.

"Good. You're very brave. Stay close by Skye and don't run off."

"I won't, James. I promise."

James jerked up in surprise. He raised an eyebrow at Skye, feeling like the little girl had just pledged her friendship to him. "All righty then, follow me."

They scuffled across the roof to a stairway. He pointed his laser down the dark shaft but sensed no movement. Glancing over his shoulder, he motioned for Skye and Carly to follow him.

Dust and ash covered the stairs in a thick carpet—looked like no one had been up here since the crash. The eerie stillness made James nervous. It was almost too easy. Surely some moonshiner lurked nearby, ready to lunge. They hadn't *all* stormed the city walls, had they?

James opened a door three levels down. They emerged into an office building with abandoned desks, cups of coffee filled with muddy sludge, and toppled papers, strewn like giant snowflakes over the carpet. Some of the doors had been forced open, and James wondered if people from the lower levels had come up to loot, or if moonshiners had stormed their way in. Someone had definitely breached security.

Drawers were pulled open and overturned, electronics and light pens sprawled on the floor. When he turned around he could see Skye's eyes alight with curiosity. It must be hard for her to resist pillaging.

"Looks like this place has already been stripped," James whispered as they scurried down the main corridor. "No use in spending time to scrounge."

"I know," Skye whispered back defensively. "I'm just keeping my eyes open. You never know when something valuable has been overlooked."

James regarded her and suppressed a smile. She must have made a successful alley rat in her day. The Radioactive Hand of Justice could have used her resourcefulness. If he could get her on that ship, they still might.

She caught him staring. "What?"

"Nothing." He shook his head and continued. He knew how much she hated gangs. Telling her she'd have had a high position in his would only make her angry. "We're almost there."

The connecting corridor from their building to the one with the energy source had been too high for the lunar freighter to hit. Usually corridors were installed at least ten levels down for security reasons, but this office building must have been a prime gathering place—maybe the city capitol itself—because corridors branched off into numerous directions from only the third level down.

They walked through the suspended corridor, where the glass walls provided a sideways view of the crashed freighter. The massive hull spanned three buildings altogether, the nose sticking into the fourth. One wing stood up like an obelisk challenging the heavens, and the other lunged into the building, tearing a hole thirty stories up. Looters had peeled away the side of the ship, the metal protruding out. Whoever wanted what was inside must have been desperate.

"Come on." James nudged Skye by placing the palm of his hand underneath her arm. "We've got to keep moving."

The corridor connected to a grand atrium guarded by bronze lions rising to a head above James. The lion on the right had a stoic, noble face framed by giant curls of mane, and the one on the left opened its saber-toothed mouth in a silent roar. The floor spread out in a carpet embroidered with green ferns to pillars carved in the likeness of vines.

Skye came up and whispered in his ear. "You think Tarzan lives here?"

James's lips curled. "Whoever it is definitely has a distinct jungle theme."

She shook her head. "Makes no sense why people chopped down the jungles in the last century if they coveted them so much. Now, anything having to do with extinct wildlife is worth a fortune."

"Too bad I'm not an aboriginal."

Skye rolled her eyes but smiled, the exact reaction he wanted. "You hardly look like one, and at this point, it wouldn't do us any good."

A stone stairway led to a greenhouse bubble at the center. The morning sun filtered down through colored glass, illuminating the lobby. Affluent higher-ups had offices even in the city's outskirts. James wondered if good-old TJ had a cousin.

There was no sign of the golden light from last night, yet James was certain this building was the source. He gestured for Skye and Carly to stand behind him and took a few steps beyond the lion's claws.

"Hello?" His voice echoed into the shadows of the ceiling.

A laser blast erupted over their heads, spewing chunks of marble and fake ferns.

Skye and Carly ducked behind the lion statue, and James held up both hands. Moonshiners didn't fire lasers. This person was still awake, still human. "Whoa! Hold your fire! We mean you no harm."

He waited. No further laser blasts came. An old man's voice wafted up from the withered greenery and James made note of the direction. "You're not moonshiners, are you?"

"No. We still have our brains, thank you very much." A pause and then, "What do you want?"

James took a step forward. "We've come to trade."

"Go away. You have nothing that I want."

James figured as much. His voice changed from authoritative to curious. "What about a ticket out of here?"

"Hmph. Don't want to leave. Now go away!"

Skye stepped out from the lion and James waved her back, but she didn't listen to him.

"Please, sir, my boyfriend's wounded and my little girl needs to rest. The city's been overrun with moonshiners, and we're fleeing the area before they nuke it to the ground. We have a hovercraft and a plan to finagle a starship out in the Barrens."

James was more shocked she'd called him her boyfriend than the fact that her words stopped the laser fire. *Surely she did it to win favor with this stranger.*

Shuffling came from the greenhouse, and brown leaves rustled. James's hand hovered over his laser. A man swung down on a vine, landing in front of them, and James whipped out his weapon as the man righted himself. His hair stood up in a wispy mess. Sharp, round hazel eyes stared back at James underneath slanted eyebrows. Smoothing down his waistcoat, the old man wrinkled his bulbous nose.

"I thought you said you mean me no harm?"

"This is just a precaution," James replied, the laser not moving a millimeter.

"It's not necessary." The man waved the laser away and looked at Skye and Carly with curiosity. "Are you going to come in or not?"

Skye gave James a questioning look and he raised his eyebrows as if to say they had no other choice. They needed his energy supply, so they had to be polite. He holstered his laser and nodded.

"Name's Charles Grant, MD." Charles offered his hand and James took it, feeling soft, wrinkly skin.

"You're a doctor?"

"Used to be." He shook Skye's hand next. Carly shook her head, and the old man settled for a wave. He led them up the stairs to a table and chairs underneath the glass dome, talking all the way. "I have to take extra precautions these days. You never know who's out pillaging. I don't get many visitors, none seeking medical attention. They're already way too gone."

The man's mouth was flying a mile a minute, and James had a billion questions on the tip of his tongue. "What happened to the outskirts?"

"Moonshine."

Charles Grant poured four glasses of water and they sat at the table as if he'd invited them over for dinner. He took a sip and cleared his throat. "People here ran out of food. Shipments stopped coming from Utopia. I heard it was blown up by a gang."

Skye looked down at the table and James put his hand on her shoulder. He looked back to the old man and prompted him on. "So where did everyone go?"

Charles Grant unbuttoned his waistcoat to join them at the table, and James marveled at how old habits died hard. Even at the end of the world, this man didn't forget his manners. "They fought over what little food we had left. People scavenged for anything they could eat, and my wife, Beatrice, and I fought them off. We have a small arsenal in here, and we used everything we got to hold them back. If it weren't for that lunar freighter crash, we would have been overrun long ago, but the ship came in and wiped out a lot of the corridors running to our building. The one you came through is about the only working one left."

"What about people coming up from the lower levels?"

"We cemented it over months ago with the good stuff that repels hypergrenades. Beatrice had a sixth sense for these types of things. She convinced me to do it way before the food shortage hit."

"Wow. So you've been stuck here ever since?"

"Not stuck. I'm here because it's the safest place to be right now, and I don't want to leave her."

He pointed to an oak box set on top of a pedestal at the far end of the atrium. Pity panged in James's chest. "I'm so sorry for your loss."

"It was her own choice, I'm afraid." Charles's face fell, his eyes watery. "When the food shortage hit, people turned to moonshine to keep their bodies going. They could subsist all day with only one dose and a pint of water. The hellish substance staved off hunger and provided the user with the energy necessary to carry on. That lunar freighter was full of it. Beatrice and I had our greenhouse, and we lived off of that for a month before the plants started to die."

His voice trailed off and James shot a look at Carly and Skye. Carly sipped her water quietly, her eyes rolling over all of the luxury, and Skye listened intently by his side.

Charles changed the subject. "Are you going to show me your injuries?"

James paused. All this time he'd been on the move, and it hadn't allowed him the time to dwell on his shoulder. Now the truth faced him like judgment day. Fear for Skye and Carly ricocheted through him. He needed to know for their sakes how much time he had left.

James nodded at Skye and she turned to the doctor, flicking a glance over at Carly. "We need something to distract her."

Charles dug into a chest and pulled out an antique box with a lens. "Here, hon, play with this."

Carly shot him a skeptical look. "What does it do?"

"It takes pictures." He pressed a button on the side and a flash startled Carly backward. A piece of paper came out the bottom and he handed it to her. "Look, here you are."

Carly stared at the paper as it dried, the image becoming clearer with each second. "Double cyber beans!"

He gave her the camera. "Here. Keep it safe for me. Make sure you take a picture of yourself."

"Thanks a million!" She darted away to the corner of the room, a flash erupting every few seconds.

Skye shouted after her, "Don't go far." She waited until the little girl was out of earshot, than turned back to Charles.

"Please, you have to help him. He's been bitten." Her voice wavered, thin as ice and about to crack. James wanted to reassure her, but he was helpless. His life rested in the doctor's hands.

"Bitten?" Charles furrowed his gray eyebrows and James could sense him calculating, holding back emotion in the trained way a doctor would. "How badly?"

James shifted in his seat. "A few times at least."

"How deep into the skin?"

James shrugged. "Half an inch?"

Skye stood up, her chair screeching backward. "Will he be okay?"

The doctor spoke in a clinical tone. "Depends on if the saliva of the moonshiner entered his body."

Skye leaned forward. "What do you mean?"

"The mineral from the moon carries a virus with it, and anyone who uses the drug will get infected. The rate of infection increases the more you use the drug. Some people can fight it off better than others. We can tell by looking at the skin around the wound. If the flesh is red and pink, he'll recover. If it's turned black, the virus has infected his bloodstream, and there's nothing I can do."

James began peeling away the layers of his shirt. He didn't want to wait to learn his fate a second longer. Skye came over and grabbed both his hands in her own. "Let me."

Her gesture made him feel like he wasn't alone. He had a partner, one to share his pain. "Thank you."

She gently unwound the torn fabric as his heart beat faster and faster until it raced out of control, like one of the moonshiners. Instead of looking down at his wound, James focused on the green flecks in her eyes. Up close, he could see hints of hazel and blue. Pretty enough to outdo the jewels on a higher-up's neck.

Her eyes widened, and she crumpled into his arms.

"What is it?" James could barely ask.

She spoke into his chest, her breath warming his skin underneath his shirt. "You're safe."

He held her close to him and buried his face into her hair, exhaling as relief flowed through him like a satisfying elixir. Never had he felt so vulnerable, so exposed, and yet so safe. "Thank you, Skye."

Chapter Twelve

Choices

Coiled tension unwound from Skye's chest as she nuzzled into James's arms. She'd avoided getting close to him for fear of losing him like she'd lost Grease. Seeing the healthy, pink skin around the puncture wounds knocked down a barrier in her heart, and her emotions flowed out unhindered.

Skye's caring for James went beyond the fact she needed him to save herself and Carly. She wanted to help him succeed and save his people. She wanted to see him reach the space station and create a safe society. Beyond that, Skye's thoughts probed into her heart. Did she want to live with him there as friends, or was it more?

As she felt his warmth against her, her emotions morphed into something much deeper, much more profound than anything she'd experienced before.

James smoothed a hand over her head and brought her closer to him, and she ached to be closer still, to feel his rigid chest against her bare skin. She had him, and this time she wouldn't allow herself to let go like she had with Grease.

"Good news, is it?" Charles asked, breaking the intensity of the moment. Skye remembered where she was and reluctantly pulled away from James. They still had a bargain to seal.

"He's okay," Skye said, as if trying to convince herself. Her fingers still shook from unwinding the fabric around his shoulder.

"Excellent. You'll be on your way, then?" The doctor handed James a fresh swath of cloth. It almost looked as though he was sad to see them go, like he enjoyed their company.

"Not yet." James covered his shoulder with the cloth. "We'd like to strike a bargain with you."

The doctor spread his hands through the air. "Like I said before, you have nothing I could possibly want."

"Well, we need a full energy cell to power our hovercraft far enough to get to the Barrens, to the transport ship. We're willing to offer you a ride out of here in return."

Charles's face was stoic. "You can have an energy cell, but I'm not going anywhere."

Skye wanted to shake some sense into him. "What do you mean? This whole place is going up in flames, and the fallout alone will kill you."

"That's what I'm betting on."

She froze, wondering if she'd heard him correctly. James shook his head. "Why?"

"I didn't finish my story." Charles pulled out a chair and sat down. "When the plants withered in the greenhouse, my wife and I had a choice: die of hunger or live off moonshine like the rest of the population. Beatrice had strict religious beliefs. She wouldn't have a drop of it. I, on the other hand, thought I could beat the substance, monitor it so that I could use it without it getting to me in the end."

Skye stood in shock, her mouth dry and empty of words. She couldn't imagine such a decision. Would she take the moonshine knowing it would turn her into a monster?

Charles pulled his arm out of his vest and started unbuttoning his shirt. "In the beginning it worked well. I took just enough to keep going and withstood the severe cravings. I could do things I hadn't been able to do in years: jumping jacks, swinging on vines. My arthritis went away. I felt phenomenal."

His fingers paused at the last button and his eyes turned cold and steely, like a winter sky without clouds. "But I realized over time I had to increase the dose to get the same effects. The virus began replicating at an exponential rate."

He pulled the shirt down, exposing a blackened chest. The skin had turned into a bruise, like old, tarnished leather. Tendrils of inky black wove around his arms and up to his neck, like snakes trying to suffocate him.

"There's no going back for me now."

Skye's stomach dropped to the rich carpet. The room felt cold and empty. These walls would be this man's tomb.

"But we have real food." She dug in her pockets and pulled out the orange she hadn't eaten from breakfast. Her voice quivered, squeezing the orange in her palm. "You could start eating again."

Charles smiled sadly. "Once you've been on Morpheus for so long, you can't go back to regular food. It changes you. Turns you into something...something else. Something that doesn't eat organic life."

James stepped forward. "Turns you into what?"

The doctor waved his hand. "I've run some DNA tests on my own blood and found foreign strands I've never seen before, not in a human or any other life form that's ever existed on this Earth."

"What are you saying?" Skye feared his answer, yet the

question popped out through her lips, almost demanding it.

"Another life form. Alien, demon, call it what you wish." He pulled his shirt back on and walked to the back of the atrium. "I don't want you to stay around to find out."

Charles returned, bringing an energy cell large enough to power the hovercraft for days. Guilt poured over Skye like sticky ooze. She couldn't accept it from him, yet she had to if she wanted to keep Carly alive.

The old man handed the energy cell to James. "Good luck. Protect your loved ones. Give them a better life."

The story she'd told Charles about them being a family wiggled in her chest like a worm. She couldn't leave this poor old man knowing she'd lied to gain his friendship. When Charles offered his hand, she refused. "I lied to you about James. He's not my boyfriend. I only said it to make you think we were a family." Tears ran down her cheeks and she slumped forward, feeling like the biggest failure in the world. "I'm not even Carly's real mother."

Charles's lips curved in an all-knowing smile. He winked, looking like the fairy godmother she never had. "Could have fooled me."

• • •

They walked back to the hovercraft with James carrying the energy cell. They'd succeeded in their mission, yet melancholy permeated their triumph like sour grapes in sweet wine.

"He's got to stay, Skye." James's eyes were silver pools of sympathy, yet no words could make her feel good about leaving the old man behind. So many people had died—Skye just wanted to save one more. Maybe she had more of James's goodwill in her than she initially thought. Maybe he'd rubbed off on her.

Wouldn't be that bad, now would it?

Skye had read something once about how lovers brought out the best qualities in their partners, how they made each other better people, and how two could make more than the sum of their parts. She studied James's profile, noticing black stubble on the hard edges of his chin. She wanted to reach out and smooth her fingers over it.

Carly ran ahead of them, clutching her new camera. Skye zapped back into mother mode. "Carls, don't go too far."

"I'm not. I just want to take a picture, that's all."

Skye looked around at the debris on the roof and the ruined horizon, full of broken buildings. "A picture of what?"

"Of James."

James froze and almost dropped the energy cell. Skye raced over and put her arms underneath the round bottom to steady it. "Of James?" She couldn't hide the incredulous tone in her voice.

"Yeah. Before we leave."

James shrugged and placed the energy cell on the cement. "Okay. Shoot away."

Carly pointed to the broken window of the shed holding the stairway they'd just come up from. "Stand over there. And smile."

James gave Skye a questioning glance and she shrugged. When Carly had her mind on something, there was no convincing her otherwise.

Carly held up the camera as James crouched down to her level, placing one shoulder on his knee. At first he gave her an awkward half grin, but then his face turned to Skye, and a real smile formed on his lips.

"One, two, three!" Carly pressed the top button, and the old device clicked and flashed. A piece of glossy paper shot out the front. Carly scooped it up. "Now we can leave."

Skye waited until James walked out of earshot to retrieve the energy cell before whispering, “Why’d you want to do that?”

“While I was taking pictures in the jungle room, the ferns made me think back to the greenhouse.” She paused, and her eyes held something Skye had never seen in them before: remorse.

Carly breathed in slowly, like before she told Skye she pulled the wires from the air ionizer for her braids. “I remember now. He saved our lives.”

Chapter Thirteen

Trap Door

The buildings in the outskirts grew farther and farther apart until real roads stretched in between them, reminding Skye of pictures from the twenty-first century. The roads widened to patches of dusty desert until there was more land than buildings, and the few structures remaining tapered off into scattered shacks.

Every dwelling looked abandoned. The absence of people prickled the back of her neck, like silence after a life of pattering rain. Skye thought she'd relish the newfound freedom of movement, but instead isolation sucked a void inside her soul.

She leaned over so far her nose touched the glass sight panel. "I thought buildings covered the whole world."

"Almost." James smiled. "These were once great lakes. I believe this one was called Lake Ontario. People built around them. When the water dried up, everyone moved east. No one wanted to build in this barren landscape. Too far from any water or food source."

"Have you been out here before?"

"No. But I've heard stories from people who have. They called it no man's land."

"Geez. Let's hope that energy cell from Charles gets us there."

"It will. The thing is bigger than the original energy cells on this ship."

James's miniscreen beeped, startling Skye back into her seat. His eyes grew intense. "This is it. We're close."

He pressed a panel and the engines died to a distant rumble as the hovercraft slowed. "Look for a shed with markings on top."

"What kind of markings?"

"Symbols in Hebrew."

Skye unbelted herself and stood up. The same dusty beige coated everything, like sand had muted the world, covering man's footprints. "Why Hebrew of all languages?"

"Project Exodus got its name from the book of Exodus, the second book of the Hebrew Bible."

"Oh." So much history, and Skye knew none of it. Her ignorance made her neck turn red with heat. Growing up in the alleys, living day by day, she couldn't have cared less about what happened on Earth a thousand years ago. Now she wished she'd paid more attention to the meager education classes in the orphanage before she left. Maybe if people cared about the past they could have fixed the future before Earth's population got out of control, before dwindling resources forced people to mine on the moon, and before they discovered Morpheus.

James must have caught her face falling because he put a hand on her arm. "Don't feel bad. I only know because I researched it on my miniscreen last night."

"It's not that. I want Carly to grow up knowing the history

of the Earth, even if she isn't on it anymore."

"I agree." James flicked a switch and the hovercraft lowered so close to the ground that sand spewed in all directions. "I'll download everything the Radioactive Hand of Justice has accumulated over the years onto the *Destiny*: movies, news broadcasts, books, everything. I heard a lot of the colony ships outlawed certain videos from Earth. But I think our people should see it all. Only by knowing our past can we improve the future."

The force of the engines uncovered a building low to the ground with a barn-shaped roof. Painted on the faded red wood were strokes of a language Skye had never seen.

"There it is. Hold on."

After checking on Carly, Skye sat in her seat and belted herself in. James landed in a swirl of sand. When the particles cleared, the building came into view twenty feet away. The ceiling was partially caved in from rotted wood. The barn looked as though it hadn't housed anything in years, never mind a secret government project.

"That's it?" Skye had expected a grand warehouse. How could they fit an entire colony ship in a thirty-foot barn?

"It's underground." James pressed a panel and powered down the hovercraft. "We have to find the secret door."

"Great," Skye huffed as she got up. "Can't make it too easy, now can they?"

James's lips curled. "I have an idea of what to look for."

"You'd better, because the clock to Doomsday is ticking."

"Finding it is the easy part." James stood up and pulled on his black cloak. "It's flying the ship that worries me."

"Oh, geez."

"I've been practicing on a flight simulator program." James sounded hopeful.

"Wonderful." Sarcasm dripped from Skye's tongue. "Now

I feel much better."

"Great, because you're going to be my copilot."

Choking back a snort of surprise, she turned to the back seat. "I'll get Carly."

Although she'd teased him, if anyone on Earth could fly a starship from practicing with a video game, she knew it was James. She swooned over him so badly, at this point, she'd follow him anywhere.

Skye swallowed down her admiration, forcing herself to look reality in the face. James had just lost Mestasis, and if she came on too strongly, he'd push her away. Besides, it was selfish to dwell on her own emotions when they had a ship to reach and people to save. Only after they'd landed on Outpost Omega could she begin to wonder if James felt anything for her.

They left the hovercraft and Skye refused to look back. The bleak horizon made her dizzy. In the city, the buildings surrounding her had kept her standing upright, and now there was no point of reference except the crumbling old barn. She squeezed Carly's hand. She had to be strong for the little girl.

James pushed open the door to the barn, and the wood squeaked on rusty hinges. Stalls lined the inside, and an old corroded scythe hung on the wall.

"This place is scary." Carly tugged on Skye's hand. "I want to go back to the hovercraft."

Skye looked at James. "You sure this is it?"

"Positive." James walked the length of the barn, opening stalls. "Look for anything that seems out of the ordinary."

Skye ran her hand over the real wood of the stall. The grainy surface felt so different than the plastic couch back in her apartment. *What would a secret door look like?*

James stomped on the floor and kicked over an old supply container. "Cyber hell! I know it's here somewhere."

Skye's gaze kept traveling to the corroded scythe on the barn wall. Only one tool, and no crops. Why would the original owners keep it?

She released Carly's hand and walked over, staring at the curved blade. The metal, although tarnished, was smooth and slick with no nicks, like it had never been used.

Skye stood on her tippy toes and wrapped her fingers around the handle. When she pulled, the scythe broke off the wall and she stumbled back underneath its weight.

"Found a new weapon?" James raised his eyebrows.

Skye opened her mouth to respond when a ticking sound came from the wall. Dust wafted up, dancing in the sunlight as the floor underneath the wall where the scythe had hung parted, the crude wood giving way to a smooth metal revealing a platform with a keypad. The buttons lit up in orange fluorescent lights.

"Looks like I found more than that," Skye whispered, still holding onto the scythe. Maybe James was right—it did make for an intimidating weapon. Although the tool was heavy, she just might keep it.

Making a broad circle around the scythe, James jumped onto the platform and brought out his miniscreen. "I developed a program that can crack the code of anything."

He flipped open the screen and a series of numbers and letters rolled by faster than Skye's eyes could decipher. The program settled on *+sl7q3]-08@h\45 rq-0P**. James hit enter, and the lights on the keypad flashed green.

James smiled. "Jump on."

Skye motioned for Carly to join them. She placed the scythe on the floor and helped the little girl down.

"You said this base was deserted?"

"Yes." James busied himself trying to find the command to lower the platform.

"Why?"

"Government stopped the project funding."

Skye shook her head. "That doesn't make sense. You'd think they'd put a life-saving colony ship first on their list."

James shrugged, his fingers flicking over the keypad. "The government works in mysterious ways. Why do you think I joined the Radioactive Hand of Justice? I've had issues with their priorities for years."

The platform began to drop and Skye shouted, "Wait!"

James pressed a button and they jerked as the platform stopped. "What is it?"

"I forgot something." Skye reached up and grabbed the handle of the scythe, dragging it across the floor.

"You're taking that with you?"

She brought it down with her. "Just a hunch."

James eyed her warily. "Watch out. You could chop someone's head off."

Skye smiled, feeling safer already. "I certainly hope so."

They descended several meters underground, and the air grew as cold as the lower levels in winter. Carly had left her jacket on the hovercraft and Skye felt like a bad mother for not thinking to bring it with them. She rubbed her free hand on the little girl's arm to generate some heat.

A beep signaled they'd reached the bottom level. Metal parted to a dimly lit corridor, illuminated by emergency lights. A crumpled white lab coat lay in a heap on the floor surrounded by broken vials. Dampness in the air clung to Skye's arms like mold on bread. The corridor reeked of decay.

"I don't like the feeling of this." Skye balked, holding the scythe in front of her, pointy end out.

James held both hands up helplessly. "There's no other way to go. They're about to nuke the city, and that hovercraft will only get us so far. Then what? Watch the fall of Earth and suffer a slow death from radiation poisoning? Huddle in some bunker for the rest of our lives?" He shook his head. "No. I refuse to go down without a fight. There're too many people out there to save. You can leave in the hovercraft and take your chances, or you can come with me."

Skye stood frozen, Carly hanging onto her leg. Everything about the place screamed danger and death, yet James was right. How far could she go in that hovercraft? And who knew what else was out there?

"I hope you'll stay with me." James's voice deepened with vulnerability, making Skye shake with need. He hadn't failed them yet.

She nodded. "Let's steal this ship and fly the hell out of here."

They followed the corridor down to a series of glass rooms. Shiny, metallic lab tables held sharp tools. Someone had bashed in the computer screens, and sparks still flew from open wires pouring out of the ceiling.

"How could looters get down here?" Skye whispered, afraid to wake up whatever might lurk in the shadows.

"Don't know." James pressed his face up against the glass. "What bothers me more is why they have labs down here in the first place. This is supposed to be a ship bay. These tools are for scientists, not engineers."

"Maybe they were working on the biodome?"

James pulled his face back from the glass and shook his head. "I saw the progress charts. Hadn't even started it yet."

A wave of uneasiness poisoned Skye's stomach. "Why would they leave the electricity on?"

"Seems like someone left in a hurry."

Skye tried one of the doors and it swung open, clanging in the dark. James shook his head. "We don't have time to explore."

Skye held up her index finger. "Just one minute. I want to look inside."

James stepped by her, his neon hair illuminating the inside of the room. A broken geode rose up from the floor, the outside rock a crumbly gray color, and the inside a sparkling silver black, dark as obsidian in the center, and white as a star along the edges. Mining tools hung on the wall: sharp and pointy drills as long as her arm, and small chisels with serrated teeth.

"What is it?" Skye held Carly back from touching it.

"It's the mineral they extract Morpheus from." James's voice was hushed, almost reverent. "I've never seen so much of it this close up." He shifted as if a snake slithered over his shoulder. "The Radioactive Hand of Justice has taken it from the Razornecks on several occasions, but all I've ever seen are crystals no bigger than a grain of sand.

Being so close to the substance that took Grease away from her sickened Skye. The longer she stared at the shimmery mineral, the more she felt drawn to feel it under her fingers. Was she any different than Grease? Or did she have the same inclinations?

No. I'm not like him. I put Carly first.

"I don't want to stay around to see what this much would do." Skye pulled on James's shirt, feeling like she should have never trespassed. "We've got a flight to catch."

Chapter Fourteen

Race

Carly's hands squeezed the back of Skye's shirt as they walked farther into the compound. The little girl shrieked and hid her head.

Skye twisted her neck to see behind her. "What is it, Carls?"

"Something moved down there."

James pointed his laser into the dim light ahead.

Skye's hand clutched the scythe so tightly she felt splinters digging into her palms. Adrenaline she'd not experienced since her alley days shot through her veins. She knew what it felt like to be watched. "What was it?"

Carly shrugged.

A shadow flickered in and out, as if someone ran from one side of the corridor to the other. James waved them back. "Let me go first."

He took one step forward as a dark-skinned man darted toward him in a blur. Carly let out a high-pitched shriek. Skye glimpsed almond-shaped eyes too big to be human and the curve of a bald, oblong head before James went down with the man in a tangle of limbs. A primal urge swelled inside her, the same urgency she had when gangmen tried to catch her in the alley. She gripped the handle of the scythe, desperation racing through her veins.

More shadows moved in the distance. Skye didn't wait to see what they looked like. She whirled around, swinging her scythe until the blade cut through flesh with a *thunk*. One of the attackers went down spewing black blood, but Skye didn't have time to examine him, or *it*. She swung again as two others reached out with fingers like wires, tickling her arms. A head went flying, and then an arm. The last attacker fell to the floor, holding its shoulder and hissing through crooked, V-shaped razor teeth.

"What are they?" Carly shrieked as Skye raised her scythe. Its eyes were dark as deep space, and no matter how closely she looked, she couldn't see her reflection. The emotionless orbs sucked in light.

James was still struggling with the first one, so Skye slashed the injured one in half to make sure it didn't go after Carly and ran to help him. Just as the moonshiner, alien, or whatever it was opened its mouth to bite his neck, James managed to regain control of the laser and fired. The skinny body weakened and stilled.

"Cyber hell." James threw the body off him and stood up. He looked around at the other three attackers on the floor and gave Skye an appraising smile. "You offed three while I battled one?"

She shrugged, although every nerve in her body twitched and her fingers shook so hard the blade of the scythe undulated in the dim light. "Like I said, I had a hunch."

Movement shuffled in the rooms behind them. James's eyes widened. "Run!"

James picked up Carly and they sprinted through the corridor to an elevator at the end. James pressed the button as Skye positioned herself in front of them, holding her scythe. Black bodies squiggling against one another crammed the corridor behind them.

Come on. Come on. Skye gritted her teeth so hard her jaw ached.

The elevator beeped and they slipped in, watching the wiry hands reach for them as the doors closed. One finger managed to thrust in, and Skye chopped it off without another thought. It plopped on the floor oozing black blood. "Where does this go?"

"I don't know. Away from here." James held onto Carly with both hands and she buried her head into his shoulder, sobbing.

"What are those things?" As the elevator moved, Skye finally released her hold on the scythe, her palms burning with heat. The blade dripped black blood onto the floor, the substance thick and sticky as caramel.

"Maybe that's what Charles meant." Even as James spoke he looked as though he couldn't believe it. But Skye could. She'd had a good look at Grease those last few days, and she'd seen the darkness in his eyes before. Grease would blink once, and there it was: cold nothingness like a black hole. He'd blink again and be back to fun-loving Grease. Skye wondered if the substance was meant to change humans as some alien way of colonizing other planets, or if the human body had a unique reaction to it.

"You think the government used people in experiments with Morpheus?"

"That or overexposure from testing turned them into those things one by one."

"I can see why they shut it down." Skye's stomach

tightened like a coil of snakes. "What if there's no ship here at all? What if it was just a cover up for these lab tests?"

"I refuse to believe it." James's voice hardened. "All of Dal's research couldn't have been wrong."

Skye held onto his hope as the elevator beeped and the doors parted again. She held up the scythe, but nothing lunged at them from the darkness. They stepped into a vast, cavernous room with wires and chains hanging from the ceiling like chandeliers. A long, torpedo-shaped vessel towered over them. Small bubble windows lined each level in rows.

James stepped closer, leaning over the railing. The silver hull reflected James's neon hair. "That's it: the *Destiny*."

"It's humongous." Never mind the space station—they could just live on that. She'd heard of cruise ships sailing in the deep ocean for years on end, but the *Destiny* loomed far larger than anything she could have ever imagined.

"It's one of the smaller ones." James paced down the balcony, taking in the length of the hull. "Holds maybe fifteen hundred, two thousand at most, if you don't mind being cramped."

Carly finally let go of Skye's leg and took a tentative step forward with wide eyes.

Behind them, scuffling echoed down the elevator shaft. Skye whirled around, poised to strike. "They're climbing down."

James pulled her backward. "We can make it in time. Come on!"

They ran across the balcony and down three flights of stairs to a platform where the ship's belly rested. A console with a thousand buttons and three panels stood by a ladder leading up to a sealed door. Finding a morsel of food in an alley Dumpster seemed easier than deciphering these controls. Skye almost pulled her hair out. "How do you open it?"

James hooked up his miniscreen. "Just give me a sec."

The elevator banged as the first few moonshiners fell on top of it. Scratching noises echoed out in the high ceilings as they clawed their way through the metal.

"What if there're more of them in the ship?"

James shook his head. "Highly unlikely. They had this project locked up pretty tight. Unless they can figure out code, which I doubt."

"Is it ready to fly? Does it have any fuel at all?"

James scanned the screen as it downloaded information from the console. "Looks good. The ship's not finished, and it won't fly us to another planet. But it can get us to the space station." James's fingers flew over his keyboard. He jabbed one last button. "There."

Streams of lights flickered on across the hull, illuminating both the inside and the outside of the ship. Air wheezed as the hatch opened, revealing a chrome interior. Skye shouted at Carly, "Climb!"

Carly scrambled to the ladder as James closed his miniscreen. The aliens broke through the roof of the elevator and moved with a strange fluid grace down the balcony. Some jumped three flights and landed upright on the ship's level.

Carly climbed one foot at a time, excruciatingly slowly. Skye suppressed the urge to rush her; she didn't want Carly slipping to her death. She clutched the scythe, reluctant to discard it but knowing she couldn't climb with the weapon. Although the weight of it felt reassuring, there were so many, she'd never be able to fight them all off. Skye threw it at the oncoming horde and the scythe clanged as it hit the floor. Defenseless, Skye sprang up the ladder. James still stood by the console, his fingers pattering over the keys.

"James, come on!"

"Just one more thing. I have to make sure the chamber will open." James pressed a few buttons on his miniscreen before slipping it into his backpack and following. Carly climbed in, wiggling on her belly, and Skye followed, pulling herself up with aching muscles. She shot her hand down to James and he grabbed on. Above them, the ceiling cracked open with a loud screech. Sand rained on their shoulders and sunlight shot down in a thin line as the two halves parted. Skye finally understood why James had taken so long. They couldn't take off with the dome still intact.

An army of the aliens filled the balcony, dropping like grasshoppers to the platform. James looked at Skye with panic in his eyes. "I have to kick the ladder out. They're too fast."

"I've got you."

Skye's grip tightened as James kicked away his support. The aliens scrambled up the slick side. Their fingers brushed James's feet as Skye pulled him up and dragged him in.

He lay on his back panting. A set of wiry fingers clung to the hatch where James had hung just a second ago. Skye kicked them away. "Close the door!"

James shot up and slammed his fist down on a panel beside the opening. The hatch shut just as a hundred pairs of black eyes stared up at Skye like minions blindly worshipping their god.

Skye fell back against the wall and slid down, their eyes burning into her retinas forever. She'd never forget the utter bleakness of a mass of souls eaten away.

Chapter Fifteen

Take off

"It's all right, Skye. We beat them. It's over." James had never seen her unravel like this. Had she given up while success loomed so close? He crouched by her and put a hand onto her shoulder. She fell forward and he held her in his arms.

"Their eyes…they reminded me of Grease."

"I know." James treaded on icy ground, knowing the wrong words would send him flinging into cold water. He knew what it was like to lose someone you loved. "You and Carly are safe now."

"I never want to see them again."

"You won't have to. When we go back to the city, you and Carly can stay on the ship. I'll need someone to work the controls."

Somehow, he'd said the wrong thing. She pulled back, her eyes bright with fear. "You're going back down into the city?" The muscles in her chin trembled.

"I have to, Skye. I need to help my people escape."

Skye nodded, swallowing hard. "I understand."

The way her voice broke on her words tore a hole in James's heart. Had she said the same thing to Grease before he left? James smoothed her hair, his hand traveling from her head to cup the back of her neck. She'd had so many wrongs in her life, and he wanted to right them all. "I'll never leave you, Skye." Not the way Grease had.

She froze, her lips parted in a question, as if she doubted his true intentions.

Why wouldn't he ever leave her? Because if they succeeded, they'd be stuck on the same space station together for the rest of their lives? Or because of something more—because of feelings he thought he'd never have again blossoming from the rawness of his broken heart. The truth knocked the air right out of his lungs.

James had feelings for Skye, and he had to show her. He had to give her something to prove he cared beyond her immediate welfare. He had to show her when all this ended, if they survived, they'd still be together, not as a gang member and his recruit, but as lovers.

Every thought in his logical mind told him to pull away. He'd loved so deeply not long ago, it was hard to imagine ever loving again. Yet this woman, beautiful, vulnerable, and strong, sat before him reaching for his love as if she needed him more than anything. He'd started as her caretaker, but she'd saved his life just as many times as he'd saved hers and had helped him achieve his goals. He couldn't have done it without her. He needed her, too.

James brushed his lips against hers in a tentative kiss. She kissed him back fiercely, pressing against him, as if releasing pent-up urges that she could no longer contain. Desire stirred inside his chest like a spark blown into a full flame.

"Yucky."

James jerked back, embarrassed. Carly sat with her little

arms crossed, clicking her tongue.

Skye laughed behind him, and when he turned back to her, a gorgeous blush brought out the freckles on her cheeks. For the first time since he'd met her, she was happy, and she'd never looked so beautiful. He had to remind himself they were still surrounded by an alien horde.

Ruffling Carly's hair, he stood up and offered Skye his hand. "Now, let's go see if we can fly this thing."

They ran through a hollow exoskeleton of a starship, a shadow of what it was dreamed to be. The floor changed from new chrome plating to metal grating, the holes so big their feet could fall through if they weren't careful. Wires hung in clumps from the unfinished ceiling, and raw circuit boards stood in place of panels. James wondered how operational such an unfinished project could be.

They ran down the length of four buildings before they found the main control chamber. Unlike the rest of the ship, this deck seemed partially finished. Control boards lit with status charts and systems operations illuminated the room. A long sight panel with glass a half meter thick ran across the front hull, providing a view of the cavernous chamber. Black shadows moved around them as the alien horde circled. There must have been three hundred of them waiting for the hatch to reopen so they could flood the ship's bowels.

How many teams had gone down to regain control of the experiment and failed?

A current of dread followed by gratitude flowed through him. He would have failed as well if it weren't for Skye and her excellent scythe-fighting skills.

Plugging in his miniscreen, James thought of Mestasis driving the *Expedition* with her mind. A control deck much like this one was her new home. Although he missed her, this time thinking of her didn't carry such a severe pang. He'd always love her, and that would never change. But his love had morphed from a tortured state to one of admiration and respect for her decision and her destiny. If she truly loved him, she'd want him to go on, and that's exactly what he planned to do. He wished Mestasis all the best, and in a way, in his inner heart, he said good-bye.

"Do you think you can fly it?" Skye asked him, studying all of the panels and charts with wide eyes.

He had no such powers as Mestasis, but he did have his miniscreen. The program Dal had made for him popped up with a click, and the parameters of the exercise adjusted to the ship, linking to the controls. He could use the flight simulator he'd been practicing on.

Confidence brimmed up inside of him and he replied, "Yes, I can."

"Good, because there's no way we're going back through those things."

James smiled. "When the engines ignite, we'll blast them all to the moon—supposedly where they came from in the first place."

He clicked a few keys on his miniscreen and turned on the ship's working systems. Low-pitched hums grew louder and higher in a drone as the ship's systems came online. They had central air ventilation, hover power, and flight speed capability—all the things they'd need for a two-day trip to Outpost Omega. What they didn't have was food. The biodome hadn't been installed, and no living quarters had been finished, but scrounging for food for a few days and sleeping on the floor were small beans compared to radiation poisoning or being burned alive.

He waited until the systems booted completely before igniting the engines. Thunderous rumbling echoed around them and the deck below their feet shook as the engines fired up.

James turned to Skye and Carly. "You might want to find a seat belt."

Two chairs flanked the commander's seat. Each one had a shoulder harness jutting out from the plastic cushion. Skye belted Carly in. "Thank goodness they finished these."

"Makes me wonder if they pushed to make the ship functional before it was finished for the very reason we're using it today."

"Good thing we got here first, then."

James pointed to the aliens squirming on the balcony like ants on crack. "I think we got here second, third, or even fourth."

"Well, I don't want to be the next person to walk those corridors," Skye said as she yanked her belt across her lap. "Nothing left to escape in."

"There'll be no one left to escape after the nuke." James pulled a lever and the hum of the engines intensified.

Skye shouted over the din, "All the more reason to leave right now."

James took her advice. Wires detached as the vessel rose up, spewing air so hot and fast it burned the aliens away in a heat wave. His seat shook underneath him, making his spine tingle and his teeth rattle as he increased the air pressure.

"You all right?" He turned his head, checking on Skye and Carly. Skye nodded, and Carly gave him a thumbs-up.

Not bad for a girl that had called him "green hair" two days ago. James smiled as the ship rose from the chamber to the broad daylight of the desert. A cloud of sand spewed up, and they rose above it until the dust settled and the shack was a dark speck in an otherwise bleached out land.

They could cover the distance to the city in half the time of the hovercraft they'd flown in to get there. James sped them forward, eager to send a message to Dal.

Chapter Sixteen

Rescue

Skye awoke to the droning hum of the *Destiny*'s engines. Red light bathed the city skyline in an ominous sunrise. Rising smoke stacks were scattered on the horizon. Her heart sped into her throat.

"Are we too late?"

James turned from his miniscreen. "No. It's gone to hell in three days."

"Do you think the moonshiners got out of control?"

"Could be." He pointed at a silver speck rising in the sky, trailing orange and gray. "Look, there's a colony ship. I hope it's not the last one."

"If they saw our ship, they'd wait to nuke the city, right?"

James shook his head. "I doubt we're on their list." He gave her a serious look. "We're taking a risk, Skye. If we can't leave before the bomb goes off…"

"We'll be fine." Skye straightened in her seat. She had full faith in James's abilities and she'd never be able to live with herself if she asked to take off and leave all those people behind. His dream had become her own. She finally understood why he couldn't have gone with Mestasis, even if he had passed the genetic test. "Just keep driving. There are a lot of people waiting for us to save them."

"Thank you for waiting." James gave her an apprehensive smile.

"Only a jerk like Thadious Legacy would leave those people behind."

James looked down at the scene. "Dal just sent me a message. He says they've collected a bunch of survivors from the city. The hard part will be getting them up here to the *Destiny*."

Skye checked on Carly, making sure she still slept. "Can you park this whale on the rooftops?"

"No. It's too heavy. It would crush the buildings and I may never get it off the ground again. We'll have to hover."

"Can they meet us on the roof?"

"Maybe. Dal says moonshiners are swarming the city. We'll have to fight them back as survivors board." James shook his head. "It won't be easy."

"Makes me wish I still had my scythe." Skye laughed.

"Oh, I've got something better than that." James flicked the miniscreen on autopilot and dug underneath his seat. Skye unbelted herself as he pulled out a laser gun twice as long as his with two pumping chambers on either side.

"It's what they call a high emission beamer. I found it on the deck while you were sleeping." He handed it to her and her arms sagged under the weight.

"You don't want it?"

"Although it fires with more power, it takes longer to shoot. I prefer my trusty old laser pistol. She's gotten me through quite a few pinches."

"What does it do?" Skye looked through the target,

focusing on a building on the horizon. Her arms molded to the length and her right finger wrapped around the trigger.

"Blows things up."

"Nice." She met his gaze and smiled.

"It's not the most romantic present anyone's ever given."

"For me, it's just right."

The miniscreen beeped, signaling their approach to the building above the Radioactive Hand of Justice headquarters. An older man's face, haloed in wispy white hair, flicked onto the video feed. "James, we're ready."

"I'll be above the roof in seconds, Dal." James saluted the screen. "As promised."

"We'll start working our way up. These buildings are infested with moonshiners, so it may take us a while to break through the lines."

"We don't have time." James's jaw was set in a grim line. "I just saw a colony ship leave. And if that's the last one…"

"We'll hustle." Dal disappeared and the screen blinked out.

James nodded to Skye. "We're going down."

Skye placed the weapon beside her seat and belted herself in. James slowed the *Destiny* to a halt above the building and incrementally decreased the air pressure on the hover drives. The skyscrapers came up so quickly, Skye worried one of them might poke a hole through the hull. The ship cast a gigantic shadow across the city. Debris sprayed up as the engines gushed air.

"How are they ever going to get past the wave of hot air?"

"Directly underneath us is totally calm, like the eye of a storm." James squinted at the miniscreen. "I'll try to get as close as I can. Looks like there's a ramp I can lower about ten meters."

Skye held on to the hand rests, feeling her stomach flip as

James navigated the air currents.

"Here. Let me set the electromagnetic field anchor." He pressed a button and the controls froze. The *Destiny* hovered in place over the city like a sleeping giant. Pulling out his laser, James gave Skye a meaningful look. "I'm going down."

Once again, Skye was torn. Stay with Carly? Or help the man she loved? A wave of nausea came over her as she thought of the day Grease left. "Won't they come to the ship?"

"I have to clear the roof. We don't want straggling moonshiners sneaking up the ramp."

As if he saw the fear in her eyes, James came over and placed his hand on top of hers. "Everything will be all right."

She'd heard that before. But the unwavering determination in James's eyes made her believe it. Skye blinked and nodded her approval. James put a gentle hand on Carly's head and smoothed back her hair.

"I promise." He took off down the corridor before Skye could summon the courage to stand up and kiss him good-bye.

Carly shifted in her seat and started snoring. Skye tapped her fingers on the hand rests, watching the city turn from dark red to orange in the glowing sunrise. She kept picturing missiles falling from the sky. The high emission beamer lay at her feet like an unused toy still wrapped in the box. She itched to go help James.

Skye no longer felt like the useless couch potato she'd turned into. Now she had a mission, a dream. She'd fought those aliens and won. She could exert her will to control her own destiny. She'd always been able to, but fear had held her back for too long. Choosing her path had brought her here: aboard a starship she thought she'd never set foot on, enacting the epic rescue mission of the century. And she wasn't about to stop toying with fate now.

Reaching across her seat, she jiggled Carly's arm. "Wake up. I need you to watch the screens while I help James."

• • •

James sprinted down the corridor feeling like every second ate a hole in his chest. Time would run out, and he didn't want the ship to leave without everyone on board. But that's exactly what would happen if the government decided to rain on his parade. He'd set his miniscreen to maneuver the ship away from the city if it picked up any missile movement from the surrounding area.

At least Skye and Carly were on board. At least they were safe. He hadn't told Skye about the miniscreen setting because he knew she'd override it and wait for him. That was one thing that differentiated Mestasis from Skye. Mestasis was practical enough to leave, and Skye was loyal enough to stay. He loved that quality about her, but he didn't want to be the reason she and Carly didn't make it out alive. If they had to, they would be forced to leave without him.

James squeezed the laser in his hand. He didn't want to face watching a colony ship sail away all over again. At least this time, if he didn't make it back, he wouldn't live long enough for it to torture him.

Stepping down unfinished stairs, he found the panel controlling the exit and he pressed the button to activate the ramp. Gears turned as the ramp lowered outside. His fingers paused over the panel to the hatch. The roof could be teeming with moonshiners, or it could be abandoned. There was only one way to find out, and he didn't want Dal opening the stairway to the wrong welcome party.

Taking a deep breath, James pressed the panel and the hatch lifted, revealing a silver walkway, built with rubber ridges like the bottom of a sneaker. James raised his laser and took the first steps down, ducking his head as he cleared the hatch.

Greenhouses filled with brown foliage lined a walkway to a building housing the elevator and emergency stairwell to the levels below. The atmosphere was still, as if the moment were frozen in time.

That's right. Eye of the storm.

James closed the hatch behind him just to be sure. The energy in the air prickled goose bumps on his neck. Office equipment, painted in red, was spread out on the cement in crude words that read SURVIVORS INSIDE. James knew Dal would never give away the coordinates of the hideout, so others had taken refuge in the building, seeking help. He wondered how long ago they'd set out their message.

If they are still alive, Dal has found them.

James stepped around a piece of a desk and tiptoed down the walkway, checking every angle. As he approached the door, the handle jiggled, and then stopped.

Is it Dal? Could he have made it to the roof this quickly?

James increased his pace, still wary of the spaces in between the greenhouses. Shadows flickered in the narrow glass window behind the door. The handle jiggled again and the door clicked, swinging open.

Moonshiners poured out onto the roof in a steady stream, each one at a different level in the transformation process. The more alien ones moved even faster than the ones that still looked human. James started to fire, and he downed the first three before more pushed through, darting between the greenhouses. They moved so quickly, he couldn't keep track of them.

Dammit!

James fired at the torrent of bodies as they poured out the

door. Some had hairless heads with skulls that extended in an oval shape and others still had braids of golden silk, their eyes and speed the only telling factor of their transformation. He fired at the moonshiners running directly at him, but his senses screamed as the others circled, closing in. The situation had gone from him having complete control to chaos, and he swore at himself for not being more careful.

Now he'd pay the price.

Moonshiners leaped on top of the greenhouses, lunging down at him with fingers turning into claws. James fired once more at the stairway, and then turned his aim at the alien bodies flinging through the air. He hit a brown-haired man wearing a tailored suit and swayed out of his direction as the man plummeted to the concrete with a *splat.*

Looking the other way, James darted between the greenhouses and kicked at the lock system. He couldn't make it back to the ship; his only chance at survival would be hiding inside. Wiry hands grabbed his arm and pulled him backward.

This is it. I've failed.

James fell and rolled, but the moonshiner scrambled on top of him. He looked into the bleak, almond-shaped eyes. It reminded him of a giant ant: drone-like and unemotional. The slit of a mouth opened, exposing crooked, pin-shaped teeth. He kicked at its body as the wiry hands wrapped around his upper arms.

The greenhouse beside him exploded into flames, shattering glass everywhere. James winced from the blast, and the hands holding him weakened. He looked up through the smoke to see a neck without a head. Another laser blast blew four moonshiners off the side of the roof. James threw the body off him and scanned the direction of the fire.

Skye stood on the platform wielding her new high emission beamer. She fired three more times before he pulled himself up and found his laser. One shot from her beamer took out five moonshiners.

She stopped firing when she saw him and shouted, "James, are you okay?"

"Thanks to you, I am." He scrambled along the side of a greenhouse, trying to get closer to the ramp. He'd have half a chance if he reached Skye.

Skye's voice cut through the din of the engines, working hard to keep the ship stable above them. "Come on, I've got you covered."

James rolled and leaped into a sprint. He felt the moonshiners gaining on his heels as Skye blasted them away again and again. Each shot took a second to power up, and that second felt like the longest moment of his life. He expected long fingers to trip him, but Skye's aim was precise.

He reached the ramp panting, his lungs raw. After her breakdown on the ship, he hadn't thought she'd ever be able to face them again, much less pick them off with a beamer. "You saved my life."

Skye shot another clump of bodies and smiled. "Now we're even."

James stood beside her, each of them firing at the oncoming horde. They backed up the ramp as the attackers closed the distance.

"There's too many of them." James didn't need a calculator to figure out the moonshiners' velocity and sheer numbers compared to the strength of their weapons.

Skye gritted her teeth. "We have to keep trying."

If they opened the hatch, they'd risk flooding the ship with the horde, leaving Carly to fend for herself and ruining everyone's transport. But if they stayed outside, they would both die within minutes. Looking at the hard set of Skye's chin, James knew she wouldn't open the hatch. They'd have to blast the devils until they overwhelmed them and hope Dal could reach Carly and the ship.

James gritted his teeth. "This might be it for us."

Skye's face was set in determination. "So be it. I'm not afraid anymore."

James squeezed the trigger, firing harder. Skye's bravery gave him courage, and he was proud to fight at the end of the world by her side.

Just as they thought the tide of bodies would never stop, gunfire erupted from the stairwell. Men poured through in the moonshiners' tracks and fired at the back of the horde.

"It's Dal." James had never been so happy to see the man in his life. "He made it up."

Members of the Radioactive Hand of Justice filed out of the door, creating a line across the roof. Half of the moonshiners broke away from the pack. They hurled themselves into the laser fire, some of them reaching the first few men in line. Every time a man went down, another took his place.

Dal shouted orders from behind the front line and the men pushed ahead.

James nudged Skye in the arm. "We're going to make it. Push the devils back into the gang members' fire."

"You got it." Skye blasted, inching forward. James's laser gun took out the stragglers, shooting them down before they got too close. A steaming pile of alien limbs mixed with semihuman parts gathered in the middle of the roof between the greenhouses. Dal crossed the distance to meet them. He pulled off a helmet and nodded to Skye. When he reached James, Dal clapped his shoulder.

"Thought I'd crash your little party."

Relief at the sight of his friend's face washed over James and he shook his hand. "You came at just the right time."

"We only made it because the ruckus of the ship drew the moonshiners up and cleared out the building. Thank you for coming back for us."

James shrugged. "It's what you raised me to do." He pointed to Skye. "You should thank her, though. She's the reason I'm still alive today."

Dal's eyebrow rose in a question and James knew the old man had put two and two together: a beautiful woman, James's new "single" status, and *voilà*. Dal laughed. "Looks like you found more than just a ship."

Skye's brow creased and James changed the subject. "How many people did you round up to save?"

"Roughly three thousand." Dal wiped sweat from his brow. "It got a little cramped down in the compound, let me tell you."

James looked up at the ship. They had about five hundred people too many. But he'd make them all fit, every last one. "And it will be cramped again until we reach Outpost Omega."

Dal waved this off. "We'll live."

Behind them, people poured onto the roof, so many that the voices of the mass rose above the hum of the ship. They carried plants from their underground facility, along with backpacks of supplies.

Dal's eyes shifted from pleased to serious. "We've got to move. There are more moonshiners where those came from. I have a team below us holding 'em back."

"I'll start getting your people on board." Skye gave Dal a nod. She broke away from them and jogged to open the hatch, ushering the first refugees onboard the *Destiny*.

Dal looked at Skye appraisingly as she left. He turned back to James. "She's a keeper, I'll tell you that. You see how she handled that beamer?"

"She doesn't want to join our gang, Dal." James smiled.

"She hates gangs."

Dal's eyes twinkled and the corner of his mouth curved up. "Joining the gang's not what I'm talking about."

Chapter Seventeen

Exodus

People shuffled by James in an endless tide as he kept watch over the rooftop. His chest swelled with pride as businessmen, vagrants, mothers, soldiers, gang members, and families of all ethnic races, ages, and social levels filed onto the ship. He'd fought for this type of world his entire life. This was the justice he'd believed in. Everyone had an equal chance of survival. In his genetic DNA book, every person on Earth was worthy to live.

Dal tapped his shoulder, bringing him out of his trance. "We're almost done. My team is on Level Forty-six, holding back the horde with hypergrenades. When everyone is on board, they'll make a run for the ship."

James nodded. "Good. I'll go down and join them."

Sirens blared like the call of lost souls all over the city, cutting through the hum of the *Destiny*'s engines. Adrenaline shot through James's veins as he scanned the sky and looked to Dal. "It's a warning. We're out of time."

Dal patted his shoulder. "You go on the ship. Prepare for

takeoff. I'll get the others."

The old man disappeared into the crowd and James's chest tightened. Would he ever see Dal again? For a second James considered going after him, but the only chance of any of them making it was if he got back on the ship.

Cursing under his breath, James pushed his way through the crowd. All he could think of was getting to his miniscreen and shutting off the autopilot mode. Dal needed more time, and he'd try to give him every last second.

Refugees cluttered the corridors of the *Destiny*, each group searching for a spot to make their own for the journey. James climbed over children playing on the metal grating and sprinted to the main control deck.

Skye waited for him, watching the city through the sight panel with nervous eyes. Carly sat belted in her seat, flipping through the pictures she'd taken on their journey.

Skye turned to him. "Thank goodness you're back. They're going to do it, aren't they?"

James reached for the miniscreen and pressed the override key. "Sounds like it."

"Is everyone on board?"

"Not quite yet."

"Cyber hell." Skye kicked her seat. "How much longer do we have?"

James had no idea, and he didn't want to have to leave Dal and the other heroes down on the rooftop to save everyone else's life. "We're going to wait as long as we can."

Skye paced the length of the sight panel, and James collapsed into the pilot's seat, rubbing his temples. He checked the status of the ship. The systems remained online. All he had to do was press a key to initiate the takeoff procedure. His finger twitched just thinking about it.

"Thank you for saving us, James." Carly's sweet voice

drew him out of his worries and James turned around. The little girl held out a picture for him, stretching her arm as far as it could reach. At first he thought she intended her present for Skye, but she looked directly at him and shook the paper.

James reached back and took the picture. The glossy sheen reflected the fluorescent light, and he tilted it to make out the image.

His own silly grin smiled back at him. He looked both overconfident and vulnerable at the same time and he wondered how the eyes of a little girl could capture so much emotion, how they could see into his soul.

James put the picture in his cloak pocket. "Thank you, Carly."

"Carls," she said. "Like how Skye says it."

James nodded very seriously. "Carls it is."

"James." Skye's voice was serious. He turned to face her, worry crawling up his back.

"What's the matter?"

"You told me the reason why you didn't make it on the *Expedition* was your heart. Are you sure you want to chance it now?"

He brought his hand to his chest, feeling his heart beat underneath his fingertips. "I'll tell you one thing, Skye. I don't want to get left behind again. It almost killed me the first time, and I know it would this time, too. My heart can't withstand losing someone I care about. Not again."

Skye put her hand over his on his chest. "But can it withstand the pressures of deep space?"

Placid calm trickled through him. He'd suspected Thadious Legacy played up his deficiency because he knew James would be a distraction to Mestasis, that good old TL never wanted him onboard in the first place. "We'll have to wait and see." He winked, trying to give her some reassurance without going into the whole Thadious Legacy conspiracy.

A beep from his miniscreen stole his attention.

Skye sprinted to him and watched over his shoulder.

Dal's face flashed on the screen, bouncing up and down as if he was running with his miniscreen. "Almost there."

James's grip on the miniscreen's frame tightened. "We're ready to go, Dal. Get your crazy radioactive butt up here."

The sirens trailed off on the video feed, and the only sound they heard was Dal's heavy breathing and the hum of the engines.

Skye's hand squeezed James's shoulder. "What does that mean?"

James's heart quickened as reality slapped him in the face. "Time's run out."

His finger paused over the buttons on his miniscreen.

Skye whispered in his ear. "Wait."

They watched Dal's video feed as he turned the camera back in front of him. The metallic hull of the ship came into view, and then the ramp. He yelled something back to his team. The lighting changed from shadowed gray to fluorescent as he entered the ship. His voice sounded haggard. "Everyone's on board."

Skye shouted, "Let's go!"

James closed the hatch, released the electromagnetic field holding them in place, and initiated the takeoff sequence.

He clicked the main intercom. "Everyone hold on. The ship's at maximum weight, so the ride will be bumpy."

The *Destiny* shuddered and groaned like a beast awakened after a long slumber. The ship rose, and the city line disappeared beneath them as they crested the layer of smog. James had watched several colony ships take off, but he'd never flown in this category of uncontrolled air space. Exhilaration pumped through him as the smog turned into white clouds. The front sight panel rose from horizontal to vertical, and gravity pressed on his chest. His heart sped and he pushed away his doubts.

"You okay?" Skye shouted from her seat.

"I'm perfectly fine." The doctors had said there was a chance his heart would weaken. Which meant there was another chance he'd survive the pressure. Breathing deeply, he increased the power of the engines and they catapulted through the atmosphere.

Behind him, Carly whooped and screamed, and Skye joined in. Finicky triumph trickled through him—they still had to clear the danger zone. Scientists hadn't tested the hull of the ship under atmospheric pressure changes.

The sight panel changed from red and orange light to the velvety darkness of space. Dizziness came over him. His miniscreen floated up and he realized he needed to activate the gravity rings. Pressing the sequence he'd learned on his flight navigator program, he crossed his fingers. Deep clunks resonated around them.

"What is that?" Skye's voice shook.

James watched his miniscreen rattle onto the controls. "It's okay. The gravity rings kicked in. We're officially cruising to the space station. Looks like at this current speed we'll reach it in two days, as planned."

James unbelted himself and tested his legs. He felt ten pounds lighter, the muscles in his legs barely working to hold him up. He had to breathe harder, but the simulated atmosphere and gravity was close enough to adjust.

He turned to Carly and Skye. "Try it!"

Carly rushed to unbuckle herself and jumped up, taking a picture of the sight panel. Skye came over and slipped her arms around his neck.

"Good job, Captain." She pressed her hand on his chest

while the other one caressed his back. "Your heart's beating strongly. Looks like you're home free."

For once in his life, James was tongue-tied.

Skye removed her hand from his chest and pressed a finger against his lips. "Shhh. You don't have to say a thing."

Before he could breathe again, she kissed him. Her lips felt soft, warm, and inviting. He put his hands around her waist and pulled her closer. Soaring feelings of desire came over him as the palms of his hands caressed her curves.

He'd given up love for his people, thinking he'd be selfish to ask for more. Now he had it all.

• • •

Skye didn't waste one second. Shyness had kept her from giving James the good-bye kiss he deserved before, but it wasn't going to hold her back now. Feeling his lips brush against hers lit her body on fire. She lowered her arms from around his neck smoothed them across his back. Every muscle tensed up underneath her touch.

Dal's voice broke her trance. "And you thought you couldn't fly this thing!"

Skye pulled away, her lips burning hot. James shook his head as if he'd been caught smooching on duty. "Great to see you, Dal."

Carly ran up to the old man and flashed her camera at him, taking his picture. "He's been practicing."

"Oh really?" Dal crouched down to her level. "And who, may I ask, are you?"

"Carly." She shook the picture until the image formed and handed him the glossy paper. Skye was surprised how much she'd warmed up to people. Perhaps after meeting those aliens, everyone else seemed tame.

"What a beautiful name. You know who you remind me of?" His eyes grew distant as they flicked toward the sight panel, and then back to her.

"Who?"

"My own grandchildren, Elsie and Louise."

Carly stood in an awkward pose, biting her fingernail. "Where are they?"

"Very, very far away." His voice turned wispy with melancholy.

"Will you ever see them again?"

"I'm afraid not. But they're in a better place now. We all are."

Skye momentarily thought of Mestasis driving her own colony ship. Were Dal's grandchildren with her? Skye's chest panged as she thought of Carly leaving on a colony ship without her. *Poor Dal.* She broke away from James and offered her hand to the old man. "I don't think we've had a chance to properly meet."

He shook her hand. "Dal's the name everyone calls me."

"And I'm Skye."

"This little cutie yours?" he asked, nodding to Carly.

Skye opened her mouth, but Carly piped in. "Yeah. Skye's like my mom."

Skye froze, her entire body blushing. *Did she say mom? Did she really mean it?*

Carly started to hum and took off toward the sight panel. Skye wanted to freeze the moment forever and keep playing it back until Carly's words sunk in. She'd actually used the word *mom.* James stared at her from across the main control deck. The curve of his lips told her she'd heard Carly right.

Dal scratched his head and turned to James. "I hate to burst our triumphant bubble here, but we've got to come up with a plan for Outpost Omega. They're not going to welcome us with open arms."

"I know." James walked over to them. "I have some ideas."

Skye placed herself between him and Dal and put her hands on her hips. "Risky ones, involving you and lasers?"

James grinned. "Those are always the best." Skye knew how much James liked lasers, but she'd almost lost him once, and she wasn't about to risk losing him again.

Dal must have seen the turmoil in her eyes because he put a gentle hand on her shoulder. "Hopefully it won't come to that."

If it did, then she'd want to fight with James. Skye turned it right back on him. "Whatever it is, I'm in."

Chapter Eighteen

Uninvited Guests

Outpost Omega started as a speck in space, smaller and duller than a distant star. Skye watched the speck grow over the course of the day, her stomach clenching and unclenching as she thought of the confrontation awaiting them. Scavenging alleys, she'd only taken what others didn't want. Tonight they'd try to take over a coveted spaceport, the final link connecting all of the colony ships.

She thought of Grease attempting to control Utopia, and wondered if he'd stewed about it as much as she worried over the Outpost. She'd turned into a gang member, whether she liked it or not, for the sole reason that she had no other choice. Outpost Omega was their last chance at a life.

Skye glanced at James as he watched news footage of Earth. His drawn face confirmed her suspicions, but she had to ask. "How bad is it?"

James rubbed his hand down his face as if to wipe off what he'd seen. "They nuked all the major cities, but the moonshiners continue to spread. Most of the news teams still broadcasting have moved to bunkers below the surface."

So much for going back to visit. "You think anyone will be left alive?"

James shrugged. "Good thing Dal thought of this starship business."

Dal harrumphed from the corner of the room. He sat on the floor teaching Carly how to play cards with a real plastic deck. "It'll only work if we can get ourselves on that little bubble of paradise. Go fish."

Carly sighed and pulled a plastic card from the stack. If it was any other day, Carly's acceptance of Dal would please Skye, but too many what-ifs plagued her mind. "You don't think they'll be willing to share with three thousand refugees, eh?"

Dal shook his head, studying his cards. James answered for him. "It doesn't matter if they are or not. It's our only chance. Dal had men pack up everything from our hideout, but we're running out of food and water. This ship didn't have much stored up, only enough for the last work crew. People are getting restless in such close quarters, and fights are starting to break out. We're going to take Outpost Omega. We have to. Hell, they may call us space pirates—I don't care. All I care about is finding a home for everyone on board. If that makes me a bad guy, so be it."

Something beeped and James turned back to his miniscreen. His expression changed from angry to apprehensive, making Skye's hair prickle on the back of her neck. "We're close enough to establish a communication channel."

Dal placed a few cards down. "Go ahead, but I think we'll have to fight our way on it." The pessimistic sound of his voice cut through Skye like a blade. "Those government bastards wouldn't let us on even if it was the end of the world." He slapped his forehead, making Carly laugh. "Oh wait. It is."

"I have to try." James's fingers danced over his keypad. He glanced at Skye and she summoned an encouraging smile.

"Here goes nothing." James opened the com link. He cleared his throat and spoke into the receiver. "This is the captain of the *USS Destiny*, requesting docking privileges."

A sharp, questioning voice shot back at him. "What is the purpose of your visit?"

James looked at Skye and Dal for the appropriate answer. Skye shrugged. Dal scratched his head.

James took a deep breath. "We're refugees from Earth seeking shelter."

Silence buzzed on the channel, weighing down Skye's shoulders.

"Access denied. This base is not a haven for the unchosen. Change course."

Skye had never heard the word *unchosen* before, and it made her feel like she had a disease.

James raised his voice, his face turning red. "There are three thousand of us with nowhere to go! Haven't you seen the news?"

"We're well aware of the current state of affairs. Our mission is to preserve the communication between the colony ships. We don't have the means to accommodate a large rescue effort."

"Resources should be split among everyone equally," James growled into the microphone, his fists bunching so tightly the skin around his knuckles turned white.

"A population that size would overextend our resources. We can't allow you to dock. We *will* use force if necessary—"

James snapped off the com link with a frown. "I've heard enough."

Skye pulled on a thread of her torn jeans, wringing it

around her finger until her skin turned pale. "So much for asking nicely. Now what?"

"Plan B." James turned to Dal. The old man had already shot up from the floor.

Dal nodded. "I'll get the gang ready."

Skye reached for her high emission beamer and clicked it on, feeling the energy chambers warm underneath her cold fingers. Adrenaline shot through her veins. "I'm coming with you."

Chapter Nineteen

Hovering City

As the *Destiny* closed in, the dome at the center of Outpost Omega rose like a gigantic snow globe, hovering in space. Underneath the glass, skyscrapers crested a treeline of birch, maple, and oak. Birds danced at the peak of the dome, reaching for the stars. Eight runways branched out from the center where ships could dock and bring in supplies.

A crash sounded above their heads, jarring Skye from the placid view. "What was that?"

James gripped the controls. "They're firing."

"Firing? At a ship with thousands of people on it?"

"They warned us." He yanked a lever down and the bridge pitched under their feet. Carly shrieked behind them and Skye ran to her, holding her close. "What are you doing?"

"Evasive maneuvers." James flipped a few switches and ran his fingers along the front panel. "Which isn't much, considering I'm flying a small city."

Another crash came from the left wing. Skye squeezed Carly against her. "Can the hull withstand these explosions?

James pulled on a lever and the bridge rose. Outpost Omega disappeared and deep space filled the viewing panel. "If I can get us high enough, we can dive and prevent a full frontal attack. There's only a certain range they can fire into before we reach the landing dock."

"Will we make it?"

James shrugged. "The ship won't look pretty, and she may never fly again."

They had nowhere else to go. They'd run out of provisions and the nearest colony planet was three hundred years away. Skye gritted her teeth. "Do it."

Her stomach flipped as the gravitational rings fought the change in forces. The explosions racked the floor under their feet, each one sending a jolt through Skye's spine. Warning alarms beeped, and the deck went dark. Emergency lights flashed on.

"We lost power in one of our engines." James's fingers moved across the panels. "I'm rerouting energy to life support systems."

"Won't that slow us down?"

"Yes. But slow and steady wins the race, right?" He gave her a half smile. "It's the only thing I can do. We don't want a fast ship with everyone on it dead."

A train of explosions pummeled the hull. Pieces of the ship flung off, and Skye held onto Carly. "Close your eyes, honey."

"They've switched to multipulse lasers." James pressed the panel with his fingertips, holding them down. "Evacuate the lowest level." His voice resonated through the main intercom. "Everyone out!"

He switched to a private intercom. "Dal, you there?"

"Yeah. Just trying to help the wounded. There isn't a medical bay anywhere on this thing, is there?"

"'Fraid not, Dal. They'll have to wait until we dock. Can you check on the lower level for me, make sure everyone has cleared out?"

"Sure thing."

James turned back to Skye. "Once it's clear, I'm going to reseal the deck above. That way they can fire at the belly of the ship all they want."

Minutes went by like hours. Skye hoped all the people they'd brought on were safe. She couldn't imagine escaping sudden apocalypse only to die on the transport ship.

Dal's voice came through the intercom. "Lower level cleared."

"Good." James's fingers flew over the panel. The engines that still worked roared in response. "We're close enough to the landing docks to dive down. Make sure you're belted in."

The dive drove all the air from Skye's lungs. She held on, wanting to meet the type of people who would fire on other human beings. She'd give them a piece of her mind, along with something else.

The ship stopped and the firing ceased as James pulled up to the nearest landing dock. "We made it. For now." He typed on his miniscreen, trying to decode the door lock.

Skye unbelted herself and glanced at Carly. Tears rolled down her pink cheeks. "I don't want you to go."

"I'm securing our home." Skye bent to her eye level. "I will come back for you; I promise."

Carly sniffed and wiped her eyes. "You're the only mom I've ever had."

Emotion crashed through Skye, overwhelming her. This was the moment she'd been waiting for ever since Grease introduced her to Carly. "And you're the only daughter I've ever had."

Skye put her arms around the little girl, and pulled her

close. Her tears fell into Carly's ponytail. They held each other until a clanking sound reverberated through the ship.

James spoke behind them. "This code isn't like anything I've seen before."

Men ran down the runway firing at the sight panel. Skye ducked before she realized they were shooting at the hatch and not the main control deck. She shielded Carly with her own body, putting the laser between them and the sight panel just in case.

Skye turned to James. "You have to think of something, because we have a welcoming crew."

His fingers sped along the keypad to his miniscreen. "The government base and the ship are simple math compared to this cryptography."

Dal came on the intercom. "Team is armed and ready to go. Waiting on you."

Skye shot a glance out the sight panel. The men were carrying large metal blocks, constructing a barricade. "Hurry, they're sealing us out."

"I need to find the cipher. I'm pretty sure about one of the pairs of algorithms, but the other alludes me."

Skye clutched her beamer to her chest, every second building her anxiety. Carly's fingernails dug through the fabric of her jeans.

"Aha! The key!" James's finger slammed the enter button, and the miniscreen charged with life. Strange strings of number and letters whizzed across the screen. "We have a way in." He stood, checking the charge on his laser.

It took every ounce of strength she had for Skye to leave Carly.

If you want her to have a better life than you did, you've got to fight for it.

Skye ran her hand over the little girl's head. "Stay in the

control chamber and watch James's miniscreen. We'll come back to get you when it's safe."

Skye expected her to argue, but Carly nodded dutifully and climbed into the captain's chair. Her little legs dangled and kicked the air. Somehow, she must have known how important this battle was. They were fighting for their right to live.

James squeezed Carly's hand and nodded to Skye. "It's time."

They filed down the corridor and met up with Dal and his crew. Fifty men and women equipped with lasers stood at attention, waiting for Dal's order. Behind them, regular citizens from the city lined up with makeshift weapons of metal beams and knives. It reminded Skye so much of Grease's failed takeover of Utopia, she had to block the memory from her mind.

James scanned the ranks. "We used to have a lot more."

Dal's face hardened. "The moonshiners took out a major chunk of our force. At least these citizens are willing to help. If anything, our sheer numbers will overwhelm them."

"Yes, but how many will have to die first?"

Dal's grip tightened on his laser. For an old man, he looked fierce. Skye wouldn't want to cross his path. "It's a sacrifice we're all willing to make."

James turned to Skye and whispered in her ear. "You're sure you want to do this?"

"You've seen my beamer skills. I'm not letting you go in without me." She had just as much a right to fight for her existence as anyone else. Skye settled a rising current of anger. He was only afraid of losing her, just as she was him.

James paused, his head so close to hers, she could hear him breathing. His lips brushed her cheek. She turned her head and met his mouth with her own, desperately seeking his attention. Their foreheads pressed together, and they breathed in and out as one. Before she could lose herself in their private world, James pulled away, giving Dal the cue to open the hatch.

Chapter Twenty

Sacrifice

Laser fire erupted from the open space, and Skye instinctively fired back. Each shot ricocheted off the metal, firing into the glass of the corridor.

"The barricade has laser repellant shields," James shouted over the din. "Firing's not going to do a whole lot."

A gangman went down beside Skye, clutching a burned hole in his chest. A rock formed inside her stomach. This was real.

I could die today.

The thought sent shivers down her spine, and she pulled the trigger harder, jerking back with each laser shot. Even the high emission beamer couldn't break through the barricade. Two more gangmen went down.

Dal shouted, "Retreat."

Skye scrambled back, feeling as though a laser would shoot through her back at any second. She rounded the corner and huddled against the curve of the corridor next to James.

"We've got to do something," James shouted over the

laser fire. "They'll storm the ship."

Dal dug in his pocket and brought a shiny orb lined with blue lights around the circumference. Skye had only seen them on the holoscreen. "You have a hypergrenade?"

He pressed the timer. "Cover me."

It was a death mission and Skye knew it. She grabbed Dal's arm and squeezed as the timer counted down. "There's got to be another way."

Dal faced her and James. Determination hardened his face. "Take care of that little girl."

Before Skye could react, he slipped from her fingers, turning the corner.

"No!" She followed him, raising her beamer and firing into the barricade, trying to draw attention away from Dal. Laser fire hit his arm, slowing him down. He pushed ahead, and another shot burned a hole in his leg.

"Dal!" Skye shrieked. She fired at the barricade until all she could see was white light. Crawling forward, Dal brought his arm back and pitched the hypergrenade in front of him. The orb flew through the air, glinting silver in the fluorescent light, like a tiny space station of its own, and landed behind the barricade.

James shouted behind her, "Cover your ears!" He threw his arms around Skye and pulled her back behind the corner. A low boom rattled her insides as a gust of searing air blew around them. Although James had covered her head, deafening silence pressed in. People opened their mouths and shouted, but Skye heard a dull ringing and nothing else.

When the air cleared, they rounded the corner. The sound came back in a rush, flooding her throbbing eardrums. Men cried for help and lasers ripped through the air. Government workers retreated deeper into the corridor. Torn pieces of metal spiraled up where the bomb had blown a hole in the barricade.

"Come on!" James gestured over his shoulder and they pushed ahead, blasting anything in their way. Dal lay face down behind three government workers firing semiautomatic pistols with antilaser shields.

Skye shouted through the commotion at James. "Dal's over here."

She fired at their feet below the shields, pushing the government workers back. As she covered James, he turned over the old man. Skye chanced a glance down and cried out. Fire blackened half of Dal's face to ash, and his eyes stared blankly at something beyond their world.

"He's gone." James's shoulders slumped forward. He clung to the old man's shirt in his fists.

"I'm so sorry." Skye put a reassuring hand on James's shoulder. She couldn't bear to think of how Dal had, just moments ago, played cards with Carly on the floor. *He'd told her to go fish.*

Skye's hands trembled as she forced herself to press on. If they grew distracted, they'd lose their advantage, and Dal's sacrifice would be for nothing.

James closed the old man's eyelids with the palm of his hand. "I shouldn't have let him go."

"He did it for all of us." Fire blasted above them and Skye ducked behind a piece of the barricade. If she didn't get James away from Dal's body, he'd be a sitting target.

"You've got to leave him."

James folded the man's hands across his chest. "He was the only family I had."

A shot whizzed by James's cheek, making a black streak in the wall above them. A current of anger rose inside her. "That's not true, James. Carly and I are your family now."

Her words brought strength back into James's eyes, and

she took the opportunity to reach out and drag him with her behind the shelter. James turned his head back to Dal and Skye wondered if he could go on.

"That's if you can find it in your heart to love again." They may die at any moment, and she had to know the truth.

The loss blinding James's eyes cleared and he looked into her gaze, grabbing her arm. "I can, Skye. I will."

Laser fire turned to fireworks around her as more of the gangmen filled the corridor. A weight lifted from her chest, dissipating in the simmering air. She nodded, swallowing tears. "We'll come back for him, I promise. But first, let's secure our new home."

They sprinted ahead, joining the gangmen pushing through the barricade. The corridor opened into a vast vaulted ceiling, painted in stars. James held up his hand, halting everyone before the entrance. "Take down those that fight against you, but leave everyone else at peace. If we are going to make this our paradise, we need to accept everyone. No prejudice, and absolutely no Morpheus."

On his signal, the Radioactive Hand of Justice infiltrated the city, followed by a stream of refugees. Snipers fired from high windows, but Dal was right: there were too many people rushing through to stop them all. Feeling as though she walked in a dream, Skye followed James down a paved street to a land reminiscent of a past century, a place she thought she'd never see.

Motorcars whizzed down paved streets. The people crossed through a garden framed by apple trees, and Skye had to tear her gaze away to keep running in a straight line. Apples hung ripening on branches, and squirrels zigzagged across their path.

James pointed above the tree line. "There! The control tower. If we can get to it, we'll take over the city."

Skye checked her beamer. The energy cell was half depleted, but she still had a few shots left. "Let's go."

People in white uniforms stopped and stared as they darted through the gardens toward the control tower.

"They're just biologists," James assured her. "They don't have guns. Keep going."

One of the white-coated men brought up a hand held mic and spoke into it as Skye stumbled over a crop of tomatoes, the ripe scent wafting up as she brushed the vines. This biodome made Thadious Legacy's greenhouse look like a child's garden.

How could these people think there weren't enough resources? Determination born of anger made her press forward. She'd secure this city and ration out the food the government hoarded. She'd make the world right again.

They reached a chain-link fence and began to climb. Behind them lasers fired through the trees. Skye glanced over her shoulder as she shoved her toe in a link for a foothold. "More guards. The biologists probably reported us."

"Must go faster!" James shouted down as he straddled the top. Skye still had two meters left to go. "They know where we're headed."

She curled her fingers around the links as she pulled herself up, hand over hand. She reached the top as James landed on the other side.

Laser fire shot around her as Skye negotiated the fall. If she landed the wrong way, she'd break her ankles.

"You can do it, Skye," James shouted as the white coats burst through the tomato patch, followed by more armed guards.

Skye jumped. The fall seemed like forever, then the ground rose quickly and she reminded herself to keep loose and bend her knees. Her feet hit the ground, sending a jolt of pain through her calves, but James forced her up. They scrambled behind a utility vehicle.

The control tower stood out like a giant mushroom surrounded by guards on all sides.

Skye chanced a look behind her. The guards had climbed the fence and were working their way down. Enemies surrounded them. "We'll never make it through."

"Oh, yes, we will."

James signaled across the courtyard and laser fire shot out from the buildings around the control tower. Some of the gangmen had made it to the center of the biodome and were waiting for his command.

The guards abandoned their posts, running at the gangmen firing in the streets. James gestured over his shoulder and they scrambled toward the door.

James stopped before they went in and Skye bumped up against him. "Hurry up. They're following us."

"Can't be too careful." He fired his laser inside at all angles and they slipped in, closing the door behind them. The antechamber was as quiet as deep space compared to the racket going on outside.

Doubt crept in at the bareness of the room and the ease with which they'd entered. "What if the main controls aren't here?" Had they just walked into a trap?

"I know they are. Dal showed me a printout."

The handle moved, and James lunged. He grabbed the handle and pushed his body against the metal, holding it in place. "Find something to brace the door."

Skye scanned the room. Nothing. The walls were bare, the floor clear. She ran to a closet on the other side and threw open the door. Large bottles of water bigger than Skye's head lay stacked in rows.

"There's nothing here."

She glanced over her shoulder. The door opened a crack and she saw the black uniforms of the station's military guards. James gritted his teeth and heaved, and the door slammed in place. He shouted, "I can't hold them back forever."

Pipes made from PVC tubing lined the wall of the closet. Skye wrapped her fingers around one and pulled. The tube didn't budge. "Cyber hell." They'd come too far to get shot down now. Skye's veins coursed with adrenaline and fear. Shot down is exactly what would happen.

"Skye, do something!"

She kicked at the bottom of the tube where it curved into the wall. The first kick did nothing, so she tried again and again until the plastic panel holding it in place cracked. She twisted the pipe until the top bent off and fell back against the inside of the closet with the pipe in her hands. The air was knocked out of her and her muscles in her back stung. Forcing herself up, she ran over to James and jabbed the pipe in the door.

James's eyes widened. "Geez, where did you get that?"

There was no time to explain. Skye wiped sweat from her forehead. "It won't hold them for long."

"We don't need forever. Just enough time to seize the controls of the city. Come on." They climbed three flights of stairs, Skye's heart pounding with each step. James whipped open a metal door.

"Freeze."

Two men stood with their hands up and conniving looks on their faces. The one on the right, a man with gray-tipped hair and a sharp nose, spoke and Skye recognized his voice from the com link. "Don't shoot." His badge read LIEUTENANT TEHON.

Everything about the situation screamed it was a trap, but Skye couldn't figure it out. Her eyes scanned the room for someone lying in wait, but the circular viewing chamber was small and choked with computer panels. There was nowhere to hide.

"Easy now," James instructed them. "We're taking over this station. If you want to join us, you're most welcome, but if you get in our way, I'll be forced to shoot."

Tension crawled up the back of Skye's neck. She watched a drop of sweat trickle down the man's cheek and wondered what thoughts flew through his mind. Would they blow up the station like Utopia and the State Building?

"I'm just following orders."

James wiggled his laser. "And if everyone else jumped into a black hole, would you jump, too?"

While James spoke, Skye noticed a strange light blinking on the panel behind the men. She didn't want to distract James, but her heart rate sped and her gut churned.

"There're too many damned people in the world," Lieutenant Tehon countered. "If everybody wanted what the higher-ups had, there'd be nothing left."

James couldn't resist arguing. "So your answer is to block them all out and watch them die?"

"Better that some live, than have everyone rot in hell," he spat.

"Who's to say what hell is?" James countered. "Aren't you playing God, then?"

Lieutenant Tehon smirked. "You watch. With three thousand refugees flooding the streets as we speak, this station will turn into a rat hole within months. Everyone will be fending for themselves. There'll be no food, no proper sanitation. We'll all die a horribly slow and foul death." The lieutenant's eyes beat down on James's. "You've killed us all."

His accusation had no effect on James. He looked the lieutenant up and down as if he were the murderer. "You have no faith in humankind."

"You gangmen have no sense of boundaries. You can't keep stealing what isn't yours."

"This is not Utopia." James clenched his fist and Skye wondered if he'd knock the man out like he had at the party. "That food resource fed everyone in New York—albeit not equally, but at least it fed them all. This space station is unattainable to anyone without the proper badge. All I'm doing is opening it to the masses. I don't want to hoard it for myself."

Skye wanted to knock some sense into James. He was philosophizing in a battle of ideals without paying attention to the flashing panels behind the lieutenant.

She stepped forward, so close that the barrel of her beamer stuck into the other man's belly. His fingers twitched as if he thought of lunging for the gun. Skye shot him a nasty look. "Don't move."

Numbers counted down next to the timer. She drew on her knowledge of computer systems. If she was right, then this man lied.

Skye took a deep breath and said, "No."

All heads turned to her. "You'd rather destroy the station than see it shared among the *unchosen*."

Lieutenant Tehon grinned. "I can't let you have it. This control tower communicates with every colony ship that's left Earth. I can't allow you to sabotage them as well."

"We're not going to. We just want a home."

James shook his laser. "Turn it off."

"All it takes is one little computer virus." The lieutenant closed his eyes. Skye's heart beat so fast it hurt.

"He's not going to tell us, Skye."

Skye turned her beamer on the controls and pulled the trigger, hoping she wasn't too late. The panels exploded behind the men, sending everyone sprawling backward. Skye tumbled down the stairs as the room sparked into flames.

She reached the bottom with her whole body aching. Her ears rang, and her head pounded. Every moment seemed like slow motion, blurred together in an incoherent dream. *James. Where's James?*

Smoke choked her and she struggled to breathe. Skye crawled over the debris across the antechamber. Large pieces of the wall had caved in, and flames blocked the stairway.

No. No. No. James had to be here. He was standing right next to her when the bomb went off. They both would have been blown back by the force.

"James!" She shouted his name over and over as the room heated up. Skye waved smoke away and saw a hand poking from a pile of rubble. She scrambled over and threw off a large piece of metal. James lay underneath, his black clothes covered in gray ash. Fear jolting her heart, Skye held his wrist, pressing her fingertips down. His pulse remained steady. She still had time to get them out.

Skye kicked at the pipe bracing the door. The smoke grew and burned her eyes, thick as a curtain. Coughing, she dropped to her back and kept kicking. The handle loosened and she shoved the door open, pulling James out.

Thank goodness no more guards were there to greet them. Skye dragged him far enough away from the burning building and began CPR.

"Come on, James."

She pounded on his chest and tried blowing more air down his throat.

"You said you'd never leave me."

James gasped in air and pulled himself up with a heave. "Where am I?"

Skye smiled, relief coursing through her. She glanced

around at the garden and the stars shining through the glass dome. "In our own paradise."

He winced as he tried to stand.

"Don't move." Skye put a hand on his chest.

His eyes flitted to the burning control tower. "The guards?"

"They're gone," she assured him. "We did it."

"You did it, Skye. You destroyed the bomb before it could kill us all. You're a hero."

Skye bent down and kissed his cheek. "I had a good teacher."

Gangmen emerged from the trees and the buildings around them, raising their lasers in salute. Two young men stepped from the crowd, laser barrels pressed against the back of an older man who looked a lot like Santa Claus in a blue suit. One of the younger men nodded to James. "It's all clear, sir. The Radioactive Hand has suppressed any opposition. We've captured the leader of Outpost Omega."

The older man's fingers shook as he reached across his rounded belly and offered his hand. "My pleasure to meet you. I'm Gregory Hollis, the elected civilian leader of Outpost Omega."

Skye helped James to his feet. He shook the older man's hand. "I didn't mean to cause such pain. I'm just looking for a place for my people." James sounded repentant, ashamed.

Relief relaxed the old man's stiff expression. He nodded, stroking his fingers through his white beard. "I've seen the news about Earth. I'm sorry the military refused your entrance. I can assure you, I had nothing to do with it."

"You didn't know Lieutenant Tehon planned to blow up the outpost?" Skye interrupted, suspicion eating a hole in her stomach.

His eyes widened. "Certainly not. If I'd have known, I'd

have staged my own rebellion."

James nodded. "The civilians will have free reign now."

Gregory Hollis blinked. "You're not going to take over?"

James shook his head. "You're in charge, right?"

"Elected by seventy-eight percent of the people."

"We'll keep you in charge." James nodded and the gangmen lowered their lasers. He stepped toward the old man. "Promise me everyone will be treated equally, with equal rations."

Gregory Hollis nodded as if he really were Santa Claus promising to give each child a toy at Christmas. "Consider it done."

After shaking the leader's hand, James took in a deep breath and saluted the young men. "Go back to the ship. Open the hatch."

The men beamed as if honored to have such a task. "Yes, sir." They jogged back to the others assembled in the main square.

James looked at Skye and shook his head. "How did you know they were going to blow it up?"

She shrugged, feeling as though she'd just been put through the recycling factory and been reshaped into a harder form she wasn't used to. "I thought of Utopia, and how the government would rather kill than share it equally."

James put his arm around her and pulled her close. "Well, whoever's left is going learn to share it now."

"I hope we have enough to go around."

"We'll work it out." James spread his arms over the vast garden stretching against the glass dome as if wanting to break free and spread into deep space. "All those colony ships are heading toward paradise, but we'll make our own paradise right here."

Epilogue

Skye adjusted the trail of her dress over the freshly cut grass. She'd never worn something so frivolous, but today she'd abandoned her scavenging rags for something they'd found in the station's antique museum. Gazing up at the twinkling backdrop of deep space, she wondered how, in all the universe, she came from the dingy, rat-infested alleys to this bubble of paradise up in the stars. She'd made her own destiny, and changed the world at the same time.

"Come on, Skye, we're going to be late." Carly pulled on her hand, holding a bouquet of real cherry blossoms. The little girl wore an embroidered, lacey dress as well, mirroring Skye like her own mini-me.

"I think he'll wait for me, but you're right." Giving Carly a wink, she led her up a hill where rows of white chairs were set up. All heads turned in their direction as light techno music drifted on a rhythmic beat. She felt like she'd fallen into some holoscreen movie, but today was all very real.

James stood at the end of the aisle dressed in a suit. Seeing him wear such formal clothes made her laugh, but when she regained her composure, she focused on how achingly handsome he looked. He'd combed back his long hair, bringing out his strong cheekbones, and his eyes stared at her intensely as if they wrapped around her soul. If two people could find love in such hardship and chaos, then there was hope for everyone left behind.

Acknowledgments

I'd like to thank my agent, Dawn Dowdle, for believing in my manuscript and finding such a wonderful publishing company. Also, thank you to Liz Pelletier and Heather Howland at Entangled Publishing. Thank you to Kerry Vail and Stacy Abrams, my eagle-eyed editors who worked so hard to polish this manuscript. My beta readers come next: the best sister in the world, Brianne Dionne, and my mom, Joanne, for giving me support and intriguing insights. My awesome critique partners deserve numerous thank yous: Cherie Reich, Theresa Milstein, Lisa Rusczyk, Kathleen S. Allen, Lindsey Duncan, and Cher Green. My flute teacher and life mentor, Peggy Vagts, comes next, for encouraging me to pursue writing and flute as dual dreams. And lastly, my husband, Chris, for allowing me the time I needed to work on edits, do research, and most of all, write.

About the Author

Aubrie Dionne is an author and flutist in New England. Her stories have appeared in *Mindflights*, *Niteblade*, *Silver Blade*, *A Fly in Amber*, and several print anthologies including *Skulls and Crossbones* by Minddancer Press; *Rise of the Necromancers* by Pill Hill Press; *Nightbird Singing in the Dead of Night* by Nightbird Publishing; *Dragontales and Mertales* by Wyvern Publications; *A Yuletide Wish* by Nightwolf Publications; and *Aurora Rising* by Aurora Wolf Publications. Her epic fantasy is published with Wyvern Publications, and several of her ebooks are published with Lyrical Press and Gypsy Shadow Publishing. When she's not writing, she plays in orchestras and teaches flute at Plymouth State University and a community music school.

http://www.authoraubrie.com

http://authoraubrie.blogspot.com

www.ingramcontent.com/pod-product-compliance
Lightning Source LLC
LaVergne TN
LVHW050959080826
845145LV00009B/2364